SCRUBBED

by

Christopher Malinger

www.christophermalinger.com

Cover design by Polar Photography
www.polarphotography.com

images provided by Shutterstock 68777212 & 361231613

ISBN: 13-978-0990701880

ISBN: 10-0990701883

DEDICATION

To Eileen

ACKNOWLEDGMENTS

Polar Photography
The Lady Lake Chapter of
The Florida Writers Association
&
The Oxford Chapter of the FWA

Shutterstock.com

Malinger Publishing

"You ask me, what do I fear?

Sir, I fear the future."

James Jeffers – *Future Madness*

Chapter 1

The desert's hotness greeted him with the intensity of a devil's forge as he exited the shelter of the prison's doorway. Shielding the sun's glare with his cupped right hand, his perspiring left hand firmly held a small tan suitcase. He moved toward the glass-enclosed transportation pavilion. He was now liberated after being "*Scrubbed.*"

His former life—deeds, family, and friends, all shades of the past, were absent, the consequence of his plea-bargain and sentence. Free and alone, he found a place to sit in the air-conditioned sanctuary and waited for his ride. He had no memory of his prior life, not even the trip to the prison. His only assurance that he made the journey came from the prison staff.

Still unaccustomed to his new identity, or for that matter, his age, he reached inside his light windbreaker and pulled out his Can-American passport. He studied it. Francis John Fitzsimons, age 35, height 5' 11'', weight 165 pounds, blood type O-positive—travel restrictions: Code B. Occupation: Literary Agent. He considered the photograph and compared it to his reflection, which stared back at him with puzzlement from the tinted-panel of the modest facility. Although the ID stated he had blue eyes and brown hair, the gray-hued glass of the enclosure prevented confirmation.

"Hello, Francis. Welcome back," he joked. He knew he was a literary agent, not because it said so on his identification card, but because he felt he was. It was an odd feeling, knowing you are someone with a particular occupation yet uncertain how you acquired those skills. Knowing you are someone with a past is another matter, and that void of recollection did come with emotional difficulties. Francis questioned if those fears would subside with time.

Francis reached into his back pocket and pulled out his wallet. His new identity included the items most people would carry to validate their being: money, credit cards, and driver's license. But it did not contain any family pictures. He had a wallet, proof he was a somebody. Again, he reassured himself. *I have a wallet and identification—I am a person.*

He turned his attention to the distant horizon that undulated under the searing rays of the sun. Rippling through the glaze of the solar radiation, something moved toward him. Slowly, the object became more discernable, morphing itself into a bullet-shaped vehicle. A low hum accompanied it along with a tail of sand, a product of its eager advance. Wheel-less, it came to a stop and hovered in place directly outside the shelter. It idled briefly, allowing its backwash to catch up, then slowly settled on the desert floor and became still.

Francis Fitzsimons remained seated, as instructed by prison staff during his debriefing before his release. The side panel of the van yawned open, and three men emerged and stepped onto the cement dock. A hooded man, flanked by two gray-uniformed men, was escorted to the door that Francis, only a short time ago, exited as a reborn citizen.

Several minutes later, the guards returned minus their charge and entered the structure that Francis dutifully waited in.

"Good afternoon, sir. May we have a look at your passport?" asked the taller of the two guards, and by the number of gold chevrons on his arm, the senior officer.

"Yes … of course" he replied.

The officer verified the plastic encapsulated document with his handheld scanner. Running his right thumb over the transparent-hologram-seal, apparently confirming it had not been tampered with, he handed it back. He said," Please, Mr. Fitzsimons, follow us."

The shorter guard directed Francis to take a seat and fasten his seatbelt. The two guards then went forward into the cockpit, leaving Francis alone. A whooshing noise accompanied the closing of the side panel. Abrupt darkness descended within the interior, causing his eyes to strain for definition. He felt the gentle lift of the craft and sensed a gradual pivot in place. The hum of the engines increased, and his body pressed into the seat as it gradually gained momentum.

Adjusting to the interior's dimness, he studied his surroundings. Glass panels, like the shelter, flanked him. Unlike those of the terminal, they were opaque. His chair was positioned between two tables, each stocked with an assortment of snacks and some printed reading material, the assumed intention—recreation during the trip. He grabbed a hologram board, adjusted the interior lighting, then settled in for the duration—to points unknown.

Chapter 2

The vehicle came to a halt. When the side door slid open, it was not in a bright setting, as Francis had imagined. Instead, the interior of the enclosure was illuminated like the transport. "Mr. Fitzsimons," the guard greeted, "I trust you had a pleasant ride?"

Francis only nodded and stepped out into what appeared to be a spacious garage. Glancing about, he noted two large closed doors at either end. His transporter faced in the opposite direction to the adjacent car.

"You will be driven to your apartment by Ms. Dasha Kozar." The guard pointed to a woman who assumed the military deportment of parade-rest. Her auburn hair, fashioned into a bun, appeared radiant. She wore a navy-blue pantsuit, tailored to reveal her curvaceous frame, with a plunging bodice. The ensemble was set off with a white collared blouse with a V-neck, which partially exposed alabaster breasts—the visible orbs clearly struggling for freedom.

With an inviting smile, she opened the rear door of the automobile and gestured for Francis to enter. "Good morning, Mr. Fitzsimons. Please, have a seat. Your destination is only a few miles away. Help yourself to the snacks and drink selections."

Francis eased himself onto the soft pile of the rear seat and stretched his legs. The sound from the closing of the door was deep—*not metallic but luxuriant*, he thought, as if a deep tone could be attached to something as mundane as a door being shut. Secure inside, the absence of outside noise made him feel entombed in an impenetrable box. The stillness, so intense, his ears craved evidence he had not suddenly gone deaf.

Breaking this seal of solitude, his chauffeur opened the driver's door, slid behind the wheel, and after another resonant closing, started the vehicle. When the car began to move, the transparent glass divider between Francis and his chauffeur slowly transformed itself into an impervious barrier—the clear glass morphing from gray into midnight black. It was now impossible for him to track his route. Trapped in a windowless mobile compartment, he had no other option but to wait until the next stop. Francis felt the vehicle surge forward, but he was uncertain of its speed.

He grabbed the holo-tablet from a nearby partition, manipulated the hovering icon, and selected the news topic. A flood of information, he somehow knew, was a concoction of useless gossip, populated the electronic manifestation. The Wall, as it was referred to, was a combination of town crier and op-ed news. His index finger swiped at the display, pushing line after line of nonsense from his sight to its computerized demise.

A couple of naked, unisex dancing mannequins pranced into view.

♫ It's time to renew and give that look the skiddoo! Don't be caught bare with last month's hair♫

He shut it off and flipped it back into its slot. He yawned.

Sitting in his shell of seclusion, he contemplated his identity. Certain things were revealed to him, such as he was ... that is, he used to be a criminal. He was given a second chance, and as part of his plea bargaining, a new life. He also knew that his crime was not something ordinary, his punishment bore that out because it was reserved for only the most major of offenses. Also, the expense involved in the process limited its use only to the most wealthy. Because of this cost, *the treatment,* as it was called, was paid for by the offender. Although the gravity of his deed had been explained, but not the specifics, the seriousness and corresponding guilt associated with it were purged from his memory.

The car stopped. His door opened, and Dasha greeted him. "I trust you had a pleasant ride, Mr. Fitzsimons?"

Francis squinted at the bright lights within the parking garage as he stepped out of the vehicle. "Yes, I did, thank you. Where are we?"

"Mr. Fitzsimons, this is your new home. I will be your guide and tutor during your transition. Please, follow me."

After a quick ride in the elevator, Francis was ushered to his new living quarters. His name, laser-etched onto a black-metallic plate, was the only identification on the door. Once inside, he eyed the spacious contemporary interior. Placing his tan suitcase to the side, he moved toward a large set of windows and surveyed the impressive nighttime view of the city. Francis, captivated by the sight, gave Dasha Kozar a brief look. "You only spoke my name in the elevator to identify our destination. What floor are we on?"

4

Dasha was standing off to the side, she, too, equally absorbed in the vista beneath them. She returned his glance. "Yes, Mr. Fitzsimons, my voice and yours are the only recognized speech patterns that will activate any of the elevators' program. Like everyone in this building, you only have access to your own level and are never allowed to travel with anyone else, besides me of course. We are on the 57th floor."

"What if I become friends with someone in this building? Will I be able to visit with them?"

"For now, whatever elevator you enter, you'll only be able to travel by yourself, or with me. And as far as interacting with others, we'll get to that later, Mr. Fitzsimons." Dasha coaxed Francis away from the window with a beckoning wave of her hand. "Come, first let me show you around your apartment. Following our tour, there are some things we need to go over before you are integrated back into society."

Chapter 3

Joe Quin conducted his trade outside the lines of conventionality. He is a rebel; a dissident who disregards the rules, thinking them only applicable to the lemmings in his world. Now, as he sits in his residence, created within the exoskeleton of an upscale apartment building, he is eating a bagel that he managed to procure from the unprotected foodstuffs of a thriving eatery.

He is thinking. He is not thinking of his repast, he is thinking of revenge. He is thinking how he can strike a blow for freedom. No, not freedom as a principle—freedom is too noble of a concept for him because he does not think of himself as a freedom fighter. He sees himself as more of an anarchist. His sense of freedom is doing whatever he wants to do. He is thinking about how he could pitch a rock into the well-oiled workings of the upper classes. Yes, he is angry, and that anger makes him dangerous.

Joe is scrupulous in keeping his castle isolated from the world. Any interloper, improbable as that could be, would see the furnishing befitting a person of high economic rank. Joe's skill in obtaining his household embellishments lay in his brashness and scheming to appropriate what others failed to guard.

His supreme talent, however, is his ability to blend into the background. As far as the government was concerned, Joe does not exist—he is without a public identity. Yes, he could be described as an urban chameleon. He is the person behind the broom that you never really look at. He is the person in the carwash as you pay more attention to your car. He is the person who picks up your trash becoming nothing more than a blur as he dumps your refuse into a foul-smelling truck.

Yet, he is more than that, He is a person who takes extra interest in his quarry. He listens to the small talk, the idle chatter of co-workers who brag about their accomplishments and self-proclaimed importance. He picks up a word or two and connects the dots. Using those markers, he develops a strategy as one might do when forming a business plan.

Joe finishes his snack and moves to a table where the contents of his cache lay sprawled, topsy-turvy, over its surface. He picks up a large cylinder that was used for records transfer and casts it aside after double-checking its interior. Memory sticks and discarded hard-drives yield the most promising results and are the first to undergo evaluation. He systematically examines the trove, an activity that will, most likely, last for several hours. Joe's business is information, and he has many customers who are willing to compensate him for those efforts. He is a techno-alchemist, who turns data into gold.

Unlike previous hauls, this is the mother lode.

Joe chooses a memory stick and looks at it with keen interest. He holds it up to the light, as a geologist would upon finding a particularly intriguing specimen. It does not glisten, but Joe knows it is precious.

"Finally, the ultimate prize," Joe proclaimed aloud to the phantoms of past endeavors that haunted his world.

Chapter 4

A gentle, persistent chime woke Francis Fitzsimons from his sleep. His eyes opened and adjusted to the gradually brightening bedroom window. The glowing numerals of the wall clock told him it is seven o'clock. A light breeze wafts over him, and contains a hint of the sea's freshness. Although miles from the ocean, the scent is meant to fabricate an illusion of a nautical air. He stretches in place and surveys his surroundings. His clothing for the day, selected before turning in for the night, is neatly hung on a nearby valet stand.

An ultra-dimensional screen sparkles to life. An eye-catching female with burgundy hair and a black body-hugging pants-suit greets Francis. "Good morning, citizens, and if you are the winner of last night's sweepstakes, you're having a fabulous start to your week. After all, one billion in Crypto credits isn't exactly subway fare."

"That's right, Zoe," a different anchor-woman announces as she fills the screen. Equally attractive, the co-anchor's hair is lime-green in contrast to her red, skin-tight attire. "Remember, it could be your lucky day, too. And, you can't win unless you buy a ticket."

The scene switches back to Zoe. "And, you don't have to worry about your safety, your identity is always protected. I still remember that awful incident in the forties. Don't you, Perera?"

A switch back to Perera. "Yes, Zoe. I remember that older couple who was killed for their winnings. An awful thing, that was. That's why, now, the winners remain anonymous."

Zoe's face popped back into view. "And speaking of anonymous, we have an emergency alert. Unidentified thieves tapped into the main pneumatic conduit and stole an undisclosed amount of records. At this point, officials are tight-lipped about the crime except that they guarantee the criminals will be apprehended. Now, back to you Perera and the weather report."

Perera stood next to a global 3D image of the earth. She pivoted the sphere until its alignment corresponds to the viewer's region. "It looks like we're in for a splendid day. I see very little—"

Francis commanded, "Victoria, shut-off the screen." He made his way toward the bathroom.

***

When Francis returned to his bedroom, he found Dasha resting at the foot of his bed. Leaning to one side, her shapely legs no longer concealed beneath yesterday's pantsuit, she propped herself against a couple of pillows. A leg pulled up slightly and over the other, she struck a seductive pose—her behavior teasing.

Francis, wrapped only in a towel around his waistline, was surprised by her presence, yet he showed little emotion. "I take it you have a key?" he muttered with a hint of irritation.

"I guess you would be correct in that assumption," she answered with a smile.

He moved farther into the room. "And that dress ... your office uniform?"

"Yes, and you will see that I replaced some of your selection in clothing. Your new office setting is quite relaxed and my choice more befitting for that situation."

"Okay, can I have some privacy? I want to get dressed."

"Go right ahead, I won't look." Dasha turned away and rolled over onto her stomach.

Francis glanced at her well-formed behind. *What's her game?*

Facing the bank of drawers set into the wall, she asked, "Mr. Fitzsimons, did you eat?"

The towel no longer covering him, Frank began to get dressed. "No. I wasn't sure what to expect today. You never really said anything about my schedule, only about the house rules. And seeing your disregard for my personal privacy, you can skip the formality of calling me, Mr. Fitzsimons. Just call me Francis ... No, better yet, call me Frank."

"Okay, Frank," she said with a smartass inflection. "We'll get something at *The Company's* cafeteria."

"Before leaving, I'd like to first make a cup of coffee."

Dasha shifted, rolled over, and turned toward Frank. "Why bother? You can make yourself one in the car." She gave Frank an approving once-over.

He was self-conscious and felt uncomfortable with her boldness. He slipped on his slacks and then his shirt. Dasha's eyes followed his every action.

"Is this part of your job—watching me dress?"

Dasha laughed. "No, just a bonus." She rolled off the bed and walked toward the doorway. "I'll be in the living room," she said, with a flirtatious lilt in her voice.

After making a few adjustments, Frank joined Dasha, who was sitting quietly on a lounger and enjoying the view. She remained reclined.

Frank approached and asked, "Where do you live?"

"Right here, in this building."

"What floor?"

"I can imagine your head is swimming with questions and that is why I'm here, to guide you through your adjustment. All your questions will be answered eventually. First, let's get going. You'll see everything fall into place once we get to your office. It's going to be a fun day."

Her promise of a fun day was not based on anything Frank could image, having no recollection of the characterization other than the raw meaning of the word. *Fun for someone may not be fun for someone else.* But, what most irked him was Dasha's evasiveness.

***

Unlike the ride to his apartment building, Dasha adjusted the windows of the car, enabling Frank to see his surroundings. While sipping his coffee, he observed his fellow commuters vying for position amid the clogged thoroughfares. Frank glanced at Dasha as she navigated effortlessly through the streets flanked by an assortment of anomalous buildings.

"You handle yourself quite well in this traffic." Frank's compulsion to engage in chitchat was more of an icebreaker than for complimentary reasons.

"Really nothing to it. The auto-features do most of the work. I'm here to make sure nothing goes wrong."

"Has anything ever gone wrong?"

Dasha looked at Frank with a know-it-all smile. "Not yet."

Her responses were always coated with a layer of sexual tension, and this forwardness affected Frank's willingness to be more accepting of her. While Frank silently searched for another topic of conversation, Dasha interrupted.

"We have arrived, Frank," she announced as their vehicle entered an underpass that soon enveloped them in darkness. The few navigational lights that were placed along their path whizzed past the windows and began to lessen as they approached a massive subterranean parking structure. The car, guided by an unseen controller, docked them into an assigned spot.

Dasha got out first and held the car door open for Frank. Before leading the way, she moved toward Frank and lowered her voice. "No one here knows of your particular situation. This corporation thinks you have been reassigned from the intellectual pool so it would be advantageous for you to keep your makeover secret."

"What about you? Who are you supposed to be?"

"As far as they are concerned, I am your academic assistant, chosen from one of the most prestigious and affluent families of Can-America."

Unconvinced by her self-appointed assertion, he eyed her distrustfully. "And how powerful is your family?

Dasha laughed. "Suffice it to say that your co-workers will be most hesitant to anger you—or me, for that matter."

Chapter 5

Frank and Dasha emerged from the garage and walked into an enormous atrium. They followed a pathway that intersected several other trails that converged at a pedestrian roundabout. Within the facility, a multitude of people scurried about, each looking intent on fulfilling some significant task. At its center, a large fountain surrounded by nine statues sprayed arcs of water into its epicenter. The idol closest to them was identified with a small stone marker and labeled Erato. She held a lyre along with a collection of arrows and bows. As they moved along the circular path, Frank took note of the other figures. Seeing the character Clio, holding a book in one hand and a clarion in the other, he understood the significance of the statuary as a tribute to the muses. Flanking the fountain were two small grassy areas with a flagpole centered in each circle. One flew the Can-America standard of a white maple leaf within its blue canton, with alternating red and white horizontal stripes inside its field. The other flag, the resurrected symbol of the women's suffragette movement, was decorated in gold, white, and blue tricolors, with eighteen blue stars running parallel to eighteen gold stars within its white center band.

Dasha turned off the ring-shaped trail and out of the maelstrom of traffic and into one of its radiating spokes toward an arched portico. Frank, in tow, eyed the surrounding buildings, fascinated by the multi-layered terraces, each with an assortment of flora that shrouded the façades with lush, emerald curtains. Overhead, the sun cast a shaft of light through the skylight, vivifying the interior of the ecosystem. The sunlight glinted off transparent tubes that linked sectors within the multiplex as projectiles, like focused atoms, darted within their clear conduits.

"I can see you are impressed," Dasha said as they entered the building.

"I am," Frank admitted.

The interior was just as enticing. Stainless steel and glass appeared to be the predominant choice for construction. After clearing security and having a light breakfast, Dasha and Frank took the elevator to Frank's new place of employment.

"I felt a lot of eyes staring at us in the cafeteria," Frank said as the indicator screen whirled through the floor numbers. It froze at twenty.

"This type of organization is a little standoffish and mistrustful of strangers. The fact that Central Consortium manages all the information for Can-America gives its members a certain amount of xenophobia." Dasha snickered. "They'll get used to you."

Stepping out onto their floor, they were greeted to an unexpected sight. Directly in front of the entrance was a statue of a semi-naked woman in a Sukhasana pose, the comfortable meditative stance for the disciples of Yoga. Frank caught Dasha looking at him. She gave him a wink. Embarrassed by the tease, he said nothing and moved on.

Beyond the image stood the entry to Frank's future. Over the doorway, symbols of fire, water, air, and earth were interwoven into a bronzed crest and bore the axiom—"Science is Truth, and only through DNA do we exist."

A male receptionist greeted them with flaunted disapproval. "Please state your business."

Dasha stepped forward and leaned down at the man who looked stunned.   "You can tell Ms. Brighton that Dasha Kozar is here."

The man's face turned red. "Dasha Kozar?"

"Yes," Dasha replied arrogantly, "the one and only."

Fumbling with his intercom, he relayed the message. Appearing unsure what he should do following that awkward exchange, he busied himself straightening his already neat desk.

Within seconds the glass door to the main entrance flew opened, and a comely brunette charged toward Dasha with an extended hand. "Ms. Kozar, it is a pleasure to meet you. My name is Samantha Brighton." She clasped hands with Dasha, giving her a hearty welcome. "Please, come in." She waved an open hand toward the door.

"Thank you, Ms. Brighton. This is Mr. Frank Fitzsimons. He will be your new chief editor."

Frank received a courteous handshake, but less welcoming than the reception Dasha received.

Dasha and Frank followed Ms. Brighton as they were led past open cubicles. Some were occupied by men engaged in examining records both on screen and on paper. A few glanced up. Frank took note that none broke a smile or acknowledged them as they passed.

Noting the frenzy of activity, Dasha remarked, "It looks like everyone is quite involved in their work."

Ms. Brighton stopped and eyed Dasha. "Last night our central pneumatic express system suffered an attack. My staff is checking what files may have been lost. The frequency of these incursions is escalating. Now that you are here, I'm hoping you will help us against these hoodlums."

"We will do what we can, *once* we are in our offices," Dasha said impatiently.

"Of course … of course. We're almost there, right this way."

After passing several more offices, Brighton announced with great pleasure, "And here is your office, Ms. Kozar."

Dasha walked around the desk and stood where the windows converged at the corner of the room. She folded her arms over her chest and surveyed the horizon. Done scanning the exterior, she said, "This will do." She turned toward Brighton and asked, "And where is Mr. Fitzsimons' office."

"I knew you wanted him to be nearby, so I put his adjacent to yours. Please, follow me." Brighton brushed past Frank and went outside and made a sharp turn toward the next office. Her movement, checked by an excited staff member, who called out.

"Ms. Brighton."

She looked at him with some annoyance."What?" she snapped.

The man self-consciously eyed the trio. He lowered his voice. "It's about that tube intrusion."

"Speak up, man." She made a sweeping gesture toward Frank and Dasha. "They are part of our team now."

Although permitted to speak, he did so with some reluctance. "I … I mean, *we* discovered which documents are missing from last night's data transfer."

Frowning, she pressed, "And?"

The man shifted in place. "This month's lottery ledger."

"Damn it." Shaking her head in wishful denial, she asked, "If that's not enough, was any other information taken?"

The man stepped back as if he anticipated a physical response. "The encrypted documents from the Brahe Project," he blurted.

Brighton's face blanched. "Shit!"

Chapter 6

Before the rays of the sun left his translucent skylight, Joe Quin awoke and began planning his evening's misadventure. Showered and dressed, he skipped his shave for the third time in a week. His new caper required the guise of a maintenance worker and the rough around the edges persona would be viewed with less suspicion.

From an assortment of name badges, he selected one. He went to his computer, which was hardwired into the proprietary matrix used solely for governmental functions. During the building's early construction, he tapped into the mainframe wiring conduit that linked most of the officials that lived within the structure. Using a pass-reader, he updated the information on the ID card and married it with the data bank of the company he intended to work for that evening. Only high-security items were transferred via the pneumatic mode. He was now Gary Duprey. He smiled at his cleverness.

***

"Where's Otto? the night forewoman asked.

"I think he's out sick," Gary said as he held his badge in front of him as it was being scanned. Gary Duprey, a.k.a. Joe Quin, posing as a food delivery man, modified a portion of Otto's meal the night before. The unique additive—a tinge of salmonella, brewed with care so as not to be lethal, only uncomfortable.

"Mount up, boys," the forewoman ordered. "Don't forget to drop your mobile phones and wrist screens into the bin inside the receptacle at the front of the vehicle."

Immediately, the cleaning crew began forming a queue in front of the transport vehicle. With his purloined identity, clearly displayed on his gray uniform, Gary slipped his way to the front of the line. He hoped to secure a place at the rear of the carriage and far away from the watchful eye of the night supervisor.

Gary located a spot and was joined by a burly co-worker whose size crowded him. Awkwardly seated between the man and the bus's frame, Gary did not engage in conversation. His rule of thumb; speak only when spoken to. Instead, he looked beyond the gray-tinted window to the nighttime lights of the city.

His ride was brief. The crew filed out, each one receiving their assignments. When it came to Gary's turn, the superintendent checked her pad. "Your badge says that you're cleared for high-security cleaning."

Gary replied proudly, "Been doing that for five years."

"Okay. Otto worked the twentieth floor—tonight it's yours." She handed Gary a card. "This is your access passcode. You'll find the cleaning cart and supplies in the utility closest near the elevator. Come down to the main floor in four hours for meal-time." The supervisor scrutinized Gary. "Do you understand?"

"Got it. See you in four hours," Gary said and gave her a wink.

Her officious manner dissolved. "Actually sooner," she chirped. "I'll be up shortly to check on you."

Chapter 7

Frank turned away from his computer screen and looked at Dasha.

"You tired?" she asked.

"Yeah," he said and rubbed his eyes. "I didn't expect my first day on the job to be so taxing."

"I think we can call it a night," she said while stretching in place. "I'm sure our efforts will make a positive impression on Ms. Brighton."

Frank pushed clear of his desk. "What I don't understand is how the pneumatic delivery system was broken into. The pressure would have changed, and because of the breach, alarms should have sounded. The security team would have converged at the rupture."

"Ms. Brighton told me earlier that the cause is still unknown. She said the entire linkage between the sending station and us is under review, and we won't know until tomorrow how it was done."

"Speaking of Ms. Brighton, she appeared quite upset being told that some of the files taken belonged to the Brahe Project. Does that mean anything to you?"

"Frank, just because of my high-ranking within the government, doesn't mean I know everything that goes on in it. It's something internal. I think she was embarrassed that the news of the breach took place in our presence. Now for more important things. I don't know about you, but I'm hungry."

Frank rose from his chair and looked at the glowing skyline. "I'm hungry, too. Do we go out to eat, or do you take me back to my apartment, and I have to order something from my AutoChef menu?"

Dasha let out a lighthearted laugh. "It'll be my treat tonight. My favorite spot, Roberto's, has the best Costata di Vitello Alla Griglia," she said with the passion of an Italian chef determined to coax the most uncertain diner into trying her handiwork.

"It sounds good, but what is it?"

She smiled. "Veal chops, marinated with herbs and garlic, and grilled to perfection with Portobello mushrooms."

"It makes my mouth water and my stomach yearn just thinking about it."

"Let's go before the cleaning crew gets here," Dasha said as she turned toward the exit. She added, somewhat sarcastically, "I can see I have a lot of work ahead of me."

Frank, getting the drift, replied, "Remember, consider it a bonus."

Dasha didn't reply, only meeting his eyes with a jovial wink. Frank, sensing a connection, began to warm up to her, but in the back of his mind, he remained suspicious.

They made their way past the empty cubicles and offices now bathed in the muted glow of the overhead security lights. When the door to the elevator opened, they encountered a janitorial worker.

The man, sporting a few days' growth of beard looked surprised. He tipped his hat in acknowledgment and stammered, "Good … good evening," and then rushed past them.

Dasha returned the greeting. She turned to Frank after the doors had closed and said, "Strange fellow, don't you think?"

"Yeah, funny you should mention that. He gave me a rather odd look."

"Maybe he's just surprised to see someone here so late," Dasha said then dropped the matter.

Chapter 8

The reflected flames from the candlelit table danced across Dasha's eyes. Frank remained impressed by her charm, confidence, and sexuality. He did not know when was the last time he slept with a woman. While part of his body expressed interest, his brain fought the urge and proposed restraint. He needed more time to sort things out.

Frank looked beyond the semicircle of the booth's enclosure. He studied the industrial brick walls and exposed beams of the restaurant. Its permo vintage bronze wall sconces created a confined glow that added more ambiance than functionality. The richly made drapes and the plush, red pile of the rug helped subdue errant conversations from other diners.

He looked back at Dasha. "How many others have you had to tutor?"

She appeared wounded and then with an impish grin she said, "Ladies don't tell, and gentlemen don't ask."

An unsettling silence followed. Frank, unsure how to respond to his insensitive remark, by Dasha's comeback, once more studied the restaurant's interior.

Dasha broke the uneasy silence."I'll tell you what, Frank. I'll give you a brief history of myself, so you can get to know me a bit more. I think that will make us better friends."

Frank, thankful for the reprieve, nodded.

"I was born in Winnipeg, Manitoba. I'll skip the exact date. Suffice it to say that it happened before the Can-America Merger. I'm an only child. My parents wanted me to succeed academically, hopefully, to carry out their own political aspirations. I became their future, so I was sent to the most prestigious schools. By the time of the formation of Can-America, I just finished college and ready to shoulder the responsibilities of a District Administrator. That may sound like a big leap to you, but my parents had a lot of pull within the new governmental assembly. My nomination was ratified without much opposition."

"I can see why the mention of your name generates the response it does," Frank said, grateful the awkwardness of his earlier comment had expired.

The waiter arrived, and with an animated technique, served the meal then departed.

Feasting his eyes on the food, Frank remarked, "It certainly looks appetizing,"

"You'll be further amazed after tasting it," Dasha confidently replied. She motioned towards Frank's plate. "It's time to enjoy the meal. I'll finish my story later."

Between bites and culinary praise, Frank and Dasha exchanged pleasantries and small talk about their first day working together. When they finished eating and dishes cleared from the table, they casually sipped their wine. Frank felt as drowsy as Dasha appeared to be.

Frank, although tired, prodded Dasha. "I am eager to hear the rest of your story. It seems strange that you went from a District Administrator to—"

"Chaperon?" Dasha interrupted and leaned in closer to the edge of the table.

"I didn't say that."

"But you think that, Frank. I can tell. Let me explain—doing what I do is my choice. This whole program that you and I are involved in is earth-shattering. When you consider the money saved and the lives rehabilitated, this program will change the world."

"Does this project have a name?"

"It's called Project Lazarus." Dasha relaxed and moved back into her seat. "To me, this is more important than running defense for partisan causes. Although, I find the political clout that I have useful when trying to get things done within the government."

"Okay, I guess I can understand your reasoning, but if you're associated with Project Lazarus, won't people know that I am part of that ... I mean, a *rehabilitated criminal*?"

Dasha let out a hearty laugh. "Nobody knows that, Frank. My involvement is off the record, and as far as everyone is concerned, I am an intermediary between the government and the oligarchy within the Federation."

"Isn't telling me this compromising your secret?"

"Frank, I'm telling you this because you're special. In your case, the term *criminal* is overstated. When you were sentenced, I wanted to be part of your rehabilitation. You have a brilliant mind, and I see great potential for it. I see us more as a team than mentor and apprentice."

"So, you know my past?"

"Not really. I only saw the physician's report. Your identity is protected, and not even I know why you were sentenced. Without that security, the whole program would disappear."

"Okay, but what will prevent someone from my past life from recognizing me?"

Dasha shook her head. "That's not likely to happen. Your domestic passport restricts travel and your past life is far removed from here."

"What's next?"

Dasha smiled. "We finish our wine, I'll tuck you in, and we go back to work tomorrow."

Frank returned the smile. "Tuck?" he asked lightheartedly.

"I only tuck on the first date, Frank."

He laughed openly.

Chapter 9

Joe raised his hand to the brim of his cap in greeting and to partially cover his face. "Good ... good evening," he mumbled as he moved outside the elevator.

Startled, Gary, a.k.a. Joe Quin tried to conceal his disbelief at seeing Rodney Bells, his one-time associate.

The woman answered with a curt, "Good evening," as they passed each other. The man merely gave Joe a nod and followed the women without showing any trace of recognition.

A rush of acid flooded Joe's stomach. Only after the elevator door closed did the sensation partially subside. *Maybe Rodney will tell the women who I am ... inform the Can-America Security Agents. Why didn't he acknowledge me? Sure, he knows that would have been bad for me. I'm boxed in. If I leave ... damn it ... I have to play this by ear.*

Joe struggled to free himself from his inaction. He had to accomplish his mission by midnight before the daily codes changed. *Because of the breach, maybe the program was changed? No, no one could expect what I'm about to do.*

He went to the janitor's closet and retrieved his cleaning gear. Realizing his supervisor expected results, Joe hurried with his cart and began to collect trash. This would help familiarize himself with the office layout and scout for the terminal he could tap into. All he needed was an operational workstation.

As Joe began, he sensed movement and the feeling of being watched. He looked over his shoulder and spotted a K5 robot. Flat at the base, its white egg-shaped top had several portals, some with camera lenses, others with undetermined functions. It approached him. "May I see your identification pass, please," it said in a mechanical tenor.

Joe stood rigid, surprised by this new development. "Err ... yes," he replied. He unfastened his pass from the lanyard around his neck and presented it to the robot.

"Please, insert your card into my reader, sir."

Joe assumed this device had some cognitive capacities. He inserted his ID into a flashing slot.

"Thank you, Mr. Duprey. You may remove your card and continue your task."

Joe, a.k.a., Gary Duprey, pulled out his card. The robot retreated a few feet and remained motionless, its indicator lights flashing periodically.

The thought that he would have an electronic snoop shadowing him proved to be unsettling by itself. Coupled with his old buddy showing up the same day as he pulled off the biggest caper of his life, proved too much to process. He moved to the next cubicle and dumped the trash container, then replaced its plastic bag. The robot followed every action. While going about his business, Joe spotted robotic vacuum cleaners foraging the carpet's surface for dirt.

Without warning, the robot left. Its absence, short-lived as it returned with the forewoman in tow. "What do you think of your helper?" the supervisor said mockingly.

"I don't like the idea of being watched."

"Yeah, that's the biggest complaint I hear from people who work on this floor. It's part of the security. You get used to it," she said with a shrug. She stood off to the side for a few minutes, watched Joe do his chores, then left without any leave-taking.

Alone again, except for the meddlesome android, Joe resumed working, always looking for his opportunity. After forty-five minutes his metallic overseer vanished. Joe looked at his watch. He saw this as an opportunity to cover more ground and seek out an open computer. Besides the mobile K5 unit, several ceiling cameras tracked his every movement. He moved with purpose but at the same time not appearing to stray from his function as a janitor. He spotted the reflection off a window from an active CPU.

At last—he found his target.

Joe considered his options. *My bubble-headed buddy is gone. How much time do I have before it returns?* He glanced at his watch and figured his electronic shadow has been gone for at least five minutes. Joe saw the office did not have a ceiling camera. He entered and performed the task of emptying the wastepaper baskets, but with extream sluggishness. He looked for a way to evade the ever-prying eyes of the security system.

As he searched, the movement of one of the programmed vacuum cleaners hurried past the doorway. It caught him by surprise. Joe's heart began to race. His head throbbed in time with his pounding heart.

I have to act now.

24

Joe's moist hand touched the glass-darkening switch on the desk's control panel and watched as the view of the inner office space faded to black. He removed his cap and from within its visor, extracted a cloned copy of Samantha Brighton's authorization card. The unit flashed. He took a pen from his pocket, unscrewed its barrel, and pulled out a memory stick. He inserted it and entered Brighton's passcode. The unit flashed again.

After a few commands, the process of downloading the daily codes began. Joe knew he couldn't stay in the office too long without arousing suspicion. He left the room and pushed his cart to the next office. Just then, his electronic busybody returned. Joe again took note of the time—fifteen minutes had elapsed since the robot's earlier exodus.

"Welcome back. Did you go for a cigarette break?" Joe mocked.

"No, sir. I'm obligated to make my rounds."

Again the admission verified cognitive interaction as well as programmed abilities. It also gave Joe an idea for the recovery of the memory stick. He glanced at his watch.

Chapter 10

Frank was not offended by Dasha's refusal for an evening drink in his apartment. In fact, the invitation was more of an obligatory social gesture on his part. Tired, he could see she was worn out as well. After spending hours together, they appeared to be running out of things to talk about, yet her flirtatious manner provided him with an incentive to perhaps make a play for her. Although many of his questions were unspoken, he didn't want to come off as being too inquisitive. After all, he knew his memory and identity were scrubbed for a reason.

He cast off his jacket onto the couch and removed his tie and shirt. Frank walked to the programmed bar and requested a double scotch, on the rocks. After giving the drink a quick taste, he reclined next to his jacket and gave a voice command to the television.

"Victoria, television game show," he commanded.

The glow from its screen permeated the interior of his living room.

It was eleven o'clock, well past the time where anyone in his zone would be competing in a game show. Nevertheless, the broadcast indicated it as being live.

The announcer, dressed in a wizard's outfit, shouted, "Who's your favorite god?"

"Zeus! Ceres! Apollo!" The shouts soon became indistinguishable.

Laughter and screams followed as the camera skimmed the studio audience. People were costumed in outlandish get-ups, each one impersonating a different god or goddess. Some had bolts of lighting radiating from their heads. Others wore white sheets with the embellishments befitting their preferred deity. They all were in a frenzy over which one would be chosen to come onto the main stage.

"Victoria, turn off the television," Frank ordered.

The transition from pandemonium to peace was abrupt. Frank stared out into the jewel-lit night of the city and reflected on his new identity. The process was voluntary, but he felt certain his decision had to be influenced by some other ruinous alternative. *What crime can be so severe as to warrant that sentence? It could have been worse since the reinstatement of the death penalty, country-wide, nearly fifty years ago.*

I gave up my life, perhaps a love, family, and friends ... for what? For freedom?

Frank took another sip of scotch. "Victoria, darken windows," he instructed the ever ready audio programmed response center. The windows promptly obscured the skyline. Frank regarded his reflection with fear. "Who are you?" he said to the replication and raised his glass toward his twin, who appeared fused into the opaque window. His double joined him in the toast.

Getting late, Frank left his partially consumed drink, along with his mirrored duplicate, and retired.

Chapter 11

Getting close to the time when the robot would make his programmed rounds, Joe Quin, a.k.a. Gary Duprey, occupied himself with the task of dusting desks. He gradually worked his way back to the office, pacing himself to be nearby when it was time to retrieve the memory stick. He looked at his watch. *Five minutes to go.*

While Joe considered the schedule, the robot suddenly took off. *Did I miscalculate? Maybe I'm not in the clear—a team of CAS agents could be on their way.*

Joe knew he had to make his move, and rapidly, without appearing to do anything out of the ordinary. He pushed his cart in front of the office door. The windows were still darkened from his last visit. He heard the sound of the robot approaching. *It has been scarcely two minutes … it couldn't have made its rounds so quickly.*

Trailing the robot was his supervisor. When she arrived, the robot took off again. Presumably, the K5 machine left to complete its scheduled patrol.

"How are you doing?" the supervisor asked.

Joe's nerves uncoiled. "Fine. I'm just tidying up the desk and cabinet surfaces."

"Oh, I should have mentioned this. In this section, the staff doesn't like anyone messing with their desks. They clean their own work areas. It's a security thing. Only do the glass windows on the cubicles."

Joe glanced through the corner of his eye and noticed the indicator lights from the CPU flashed periodically, signaling the completion of the download. He moved from the doorway to deflect attention away from the interior.

He gave her a forced laugh. "That explains why I didn't have so much to do."

She smiled. "Gary, I see that you are well-organized. I am impressed with your proficiency. I know this is only a temporary assignment for you, but would you consider working with my crew on a full-time basis?"

I didn't see this coming. He shrugged. "I'll have to think about it, but thank you for the compliment."

"You're not like the rest of my crew ... you seem to ... have a lot more on the ball." She gave Joe a playful smile. "Of course, you already have the clearance for this type of duty, so you would have to ..." She let her comment hang in mid-sentence. "By the way, my name is Marcie ... Marcie Reynolds." She extended a hand.

Joe took off his latex gloves. He wiped off the dampness from his hand on the side of his trouser and accepted. "Well, you already know my name from the assignment roster, but to make our acquaintance official, ... err, Gary Duprey. Pleased to meet you, Ms. Reynolds," he said riveting his eyes to hers.

With their working relationship cemented, Joe became anxious. "I really should get back to work," he said with apologetic gusto, gilded in feigned charm. His eye contact with her sparkled with sexual temptation.

"Of course." Noticeably taken, Marcie said invitingly, "I'll see you in the main lobby in a couple of hours."

Joe knew the power of flirtation when it suited his purposes. He confirmed the time with a beguiling grin. "In a couple of hours."

Now alone, Joe realized the robot would be arriving any minute. *If I just remove the memory stick without the eject command, the unit will protest with an audible ping.*

Joe heard the whirling sound of the K5 unit approach. His customary cool-headedness was absent, panic began to set in again. Joe then understood all he had to do was block the door. He pulled his cart into the doorway, making it impossible for his unwanted companion to enter.

With the view from the outside blocked by the cart, and the windows darkened, he was free to proceed, uninterrupted, and in complete privacy. Joe went to the desk, gave the command to eject, and pulled out the memory stick. He then slid the stick into his hollowed-out pen and put it back into his breast pocket.

"Please, remove your cart from the doorway, Mr. Duprey."

"Yes ... yes, I'm coming," he replied but froze halfway to the door. He forgot to remove the cloned ID card from the CPU.

"Please, remove your cart from the doorway, Mr. Duprey."

"I'm coming, I'm coming. Keep your metal pants on." Joe pulled out the card and started for the door. Aided by the K5 unit, the cart began to move into the room.

"Mr. Duprey, you are in violation of fire regulations. All doorways must remain unrestricted. Please, remove your cart from the doorway."

Joe grabbed the cart's handle and pulled it free of the opening and allowed the robot to enter the room. It made a complete trip around the interior, its round top scanning the office, presumably for any infractions.

"I'm done," Joe said indifferently. He spitefully switched off the lights, leaving the robot in the dark, and returned the windows to their original state of transparency.

***

Joe gathered with the rest of the cleaning staff in the lobby on the first floor. Besides the maintenance crew, a couple of security guards stationed themselves at their post behind a curved reception desk. One of the guards eyed the collection with distrust, a look that Joe was only too familiar with. Joe tried to avoid direct eye contact.

Because of its size, the groups were divided into two parties before going into the elevator to the cafeteria. Marcie Reynolds remained in the second group, along with Joe. She stood near him and conveyed her interest with a teasing smile.

What the Hell, I'll play your game. Joe repaid the look with a glow of mutual attraction.

Marcie received her meal first and moved to the rear of the dining hall. As Joe searched for a suitable location, he caught Marcie giving him a wave. With some hesitation, he followed her direction. As he approached her table, he could sense the piercing gaze of his fellow workers.

She motioned. "Have a seat."

Gary, the imposter, accepted the invitation, but the genuine Joe remained curious about her intentions. He was about due for a new sexual adventure and presumed that her interest remained more or less along those lines. His last tryst involved an engineer who worked for the transit authority. Her motives were transparent—one-time sexual release. He assumed this would be the same.

He sat down on the chair opposite hers. "Won't your crew find it odd that I'm sitting with you?

"They do what I say and don't question anything."

Joe, surprised by her candor, smiled.

Marcie poked at her salad. "What's your story. This is the first time you filled in for anyone. Usually, it's someone that's been here before."

Joe felt uncomfortable. His *modus operandi* was more indirect. He preferred, for the most part, the facelessness of working within the shadows. Now, he had a sneaking suspicion of being interrogated, albeit with a velvet touch. "I've been with *The Company* several years, but only recently transferred to this region."

Needing to interrupt her focus on him, Joe countered, "What about you? How did you end up doing … this?" He waved his hand toward the group.

Joe immediately regretted the inference that Marcie's position was less than optimal.

She gave him a glassy stare. "Do you think this is a second-rate position? I had to compete against at least two hundred applicants." She put down her fork and folded her arms over her chest.

"No … no, I didn't mean to imply that. You're beautiful and refined. I only thought—"

"You probably should quit there." She let her arms relax onto her lap and a small smile formed on her face. "Thank you. It's that damn quota system. We, women, have overcome years of prejudice. Even though we occupy most of the positions of power, there is still discrimination within our ranks. It's all about who you know."

"Where do you live?" Marcie asked as she resumed nibbling on her meal. To Joe, it was apparent she did not hold onto anger.

That question never surprised Joe, because it was one of the most familiar when he connected with the opposite sex. "A small apartment near the river district." He added self-consciously, "It suits me." He did have a place, but it was more of a decoy. Living the life he had chosen, the trappings of a conformist were necessary. Although admitting he had a place, he seldom spent more than a week or two in it on any given month.

"I guess it's my turn. No need to apologize. I assume you have applied for housing arrangements with *The Company*?"

"Like I said, I'm new to the area. My name is registered with the housing authority. I can put up with the cramped quarters until my number comes up." The fact is, he hadn't. If he put his name into any network, it would give him a public profile—something he did not want. In fact, he managed to keep off all public records, including the face recognition programs.

When they finished eating, Marcie rose and reached over the table and playfully plucked Joe's pen from his breast pocket. She grabbed a napkin off the dispenser. "Here's my phone number. You can copy it into your contact list at the end of the shift when I return your phone." She pressed down on the push button, and the tip failed to eject.

CHAPTER 12

Marcie's action was unexpected and too quick for Joe to intercept. He reached out to grab his pen. "I've been meaning to get a replacement cartridge," he said while she hesitated in surrendering it.

"It's a nice pen," she said, admiring it with unusual interest.

Joe continued to hold out his hand. "It has sentimental value."

Marcie relinquished the pen. "A girlfriend?"

Joe thought the acknowledgment of a past love would require more of an explanation. "No, I got it from my parents several years ago."

"No matter." She reached into the inside pocket of her uniform's vest and produced her own pen. She jotted down her number onto the napkin and invitingly stuffed it into Joe's breast pocket. "There, now you know how to get in touch with me." It was apparent, by her unabashed display, that Marcie had one thing in mind.

He patted his pocket. "You can count on it."

Smiling, Marcie strolled past Joe and signaled for the crew to get back to work. He studied her backside as she moved unhurriedly toward the exit.

***

Back on his floor and shadowed by his wheeled automaton, he went through the motions of his adopted profession. Having been cautioned against cleaning the desks, he busied himself wiping the glass surfaces around the cubicles and office windows. This was not a meaningless endeavor for him—for it gave him an opportunity at collecting other tidbits of information. A carelessly discarded note was always a prize, and Joe's eidetic memory easily retained its essence. No matter the mandatory directives regarding protecting sensitive material, there was still someone who would become lazy, negligent or downright stupid. That was priceless thinking for a man who lived to steal.

Following a few regular programmed absences, the robot took off unexpectantly. Marcie trailed a few steps behind when it returned.   Joe placed his spray cleaner and rag on the desk within the cubicle he had been working in.

She gave a quick assessment of the immediate area. "Looks like you're about done. Otto is a bit slower."

"Yeah, I guess I wasn't sure how long this job would take, so I pushed myself."

Marcie leaned back and partially sat on the nearby desk. "What do you do when you get off?"

"Whaddaya mean by, *do?*" Joe asked.

"You know, get something to eat or ... drink."

"Sometimes one or the other, or both."

"No matter, I know a place where the music is raw, and the drinks are stiff."

"This place, is it off the grid and free from CAS control?"

"It's called Rickey's, No one can go there unless you're invited. And I'm inviting you now."

Joe, a.k.a. Gary, placed his hands on his hips. "Before going out, I usually go first to my apartment to change."

Marcie moved away from her perch and faced him. "I'll follow you to your place, then we'll go to Rickey's." She stroked Joe's shoulder before she began to leave.

"This place, Rickey's, is it open at five in the morning?"

She turned toward him and smiled. "Rickey's is always open. See you at the end of our shift." Then with the gracefulness of a panther, she departed.

Once more, Joe considered Marcie's behind with growing interest.

***

Joe reached around the door frame and switched on the lights to his apartment. "You can put your bag over therer," he said, motioning toward a newer looking leather chair.

"Okay, but I would like to get out of these work clothes."

"Sure thing. The bathroom is over there." Joe made a quick gesture toward a partially opened door.

While Marcie changed, Joe went into his bedroom and swapped his work outfit for a pullover and jeans. He returned with his uniform in hand and draped it over a kitchen chair. He then went to the refrigerator, a holdover from a decade ago, which was probably viewed by most as an antique. Except for a bottle of scotch and brandy, it was empty. He called out, "You like your scotch on the rocks, or neat?"

Marcie opened the bathroom door. "However you drink it is fine with me."

"I favor mine with a chill," he remarked offhandedly.

From the frost-laden freezer, he popped a few ice cubes into a pair of glasses.

When she came into full view, she was wearing knee-high boots, a skin-tight body stocking, and a loose-fitting, see-through top—inflaming his desire. Marcie's coordinated black outfit accentuated her catlike gracefulness as she moved closer.

Joe froze, his attention fixed on Marcie's breasts. He held the bottle, hesitating for a moment, before breaking his focus. He set the scotch aside. Drawing near, she beckoned to him with open arms. He pulled her close, and their lips met, locking themselves into a long and passionate kiss.

Marcie pulled back. "Not that I don't want to," she said with some reluctance and breaking the mood, "but it took me a while to get into this outfit. I'd like to unwind first. How about saving our drinks for Rickey's?"

Joe agreed with a reluctant nod and retreated back to the counter. "Well, let's get going," he said as he put the bottle back in the refrigerator.

Marcie caught a glimpse of the inside. "You don't appear to have any food on hand."

Joe closed the door and turned toward her. "Yeah, I really don't do a lot of cooking. I mostly go out to eat." He started for the door.

She followed his lead. "I'd say it looks like you don't do any cooking."

***

35

Marcie drove through the labyrinth of alleys and narrow streets of Old Town before coming to a nondescript building that masqueraded itself as a warehouse. Rickey's was one of those obscure places that only the in-the-know could find.

They let themselves in through a door on the loading dock. Marcie and Joe then followed a twisted route that eventually brought them to an office door. Once inside, they were greeted by a male switchboard operator who sat behind a massive desk. "May I help you?" the man asked.

Without a bit of hesitation, Marcie spoke up. "We're looking for a safe house."

The operator reached under his console. Responding to a vague buzzing noise, one of the paneled walls slid open to reveal the entrance to a dimly lit passageway. Marcie took the lead and proceeded into its secretive void. Joe followed. As they traveled down the hallway, a jarring racket, competed with the pulsating sound of a throbbing drum began to grow louder. When they reached the end of the seemingly limitless corridor, another section of the wall gave way to an explosion of light and thunderous music.

Joe gawked at the throng of animated revelers. Their numbers, although great, were masked by the flashing strobe lights. Marcie grabbed Joe and pulled him into the whirl of frolicking-dervishes who gyrated around the dance-floor in a swirling mass. Joe, now joined to Marcie, became one with the gathering. She drew him closer, laughing at his confusion. After teasing him with her come-hither eyes, she playfully released her hold. Joe staggered backward before Marcie reached out to help him regain his footing. Their eyes met again. Joe felt a surge of desire he had never felt before. He had never met a woman more spontaneous or irresistible. He wanted her.

CHAPTER 13

Looking beyond the glass and stainless façade, Frank and Dasha could see that they were walking into a hive of activity. Even the normally indifferent receptionist appeared engaged in a task. He looked up, gave them a nod, and reached for the intercom.

"Don't bother," Dasha said, as she strolled past.

Frank caught a hint, out of the corner of his eye, that Dasha's order was being ignored.

Samantha Brighton intercepted them as they made their way to their offices. "Things aren't always as hectic as this," she said with a slight blush. "All of our staff are involved in trying to locate the break-in point of our pneumatic security system." Her behavior apologetic, she acted more like a subordinate enlightening a supervisor of an offense.

Dasha appeared to take the update in stride. "I'm sure they will find the point of the breach, but that's not going to tell us who did this."

Brighton's voice rose defensively. "Yes, of course. But we're hoping to find some clue as to who the culprit is. After we locate the break and check the security cameras in the area, we'll have more evidence as to whom we are dealing with."

Dasha backed down. "Yes … yes, of course, you're right, Ms. Brighton. Once you have that information, I would be most interested in hearing more."

Frank could see the developing tension between the two women and gave only a passing nod to Brighton as they continued on to their offices.

"She resents me," Dasha commented once they were out of earshot. "The fact is, she may be our boss, but she knows I have more political clout—that sticks in her craw."

"It 's not a good idea to poke a caged lion, or in this case, a lioness, "said Frank lightheartedly. "Someday she may be on the outside of that cage."

"I knew you were a smart one, Frank. We'll get along just fine." Dasha patted him on his shoulder as they entered his office.

Dasha took note of the CPU. "I see that you forgot to turn off your unit," she said, pointing toward the bright indicator lamp. "Security protocol's demand that all computers be turned off. I'm not going to make an issue of it because you're new but, more careful in the future."

Not liking the reprimand, Frank only said, "I understand."

"Yesterday was only a warm-up," Dasha said as she sat down. She patted the chair next to her. "Have a seat. Now we'll get into the heart of your job. Because of your inherent skills, you'll be checking the content of all Class One documents for possible conflicts with state protocols."

Frank sat down. "How am I going to know that? I may be able to understand sentence structure and verbal expression, but regulations … that's another matter."

"That's why I'm here, Frank. Now let's get going—lesson one." She drew closer to Frank and logged onto the computer.

***

Ms. Brighton stood in the doorway and announced herself by clearing her throat. "I have news on that incident." Without an invitation, she moved to one of the side chairs along the wall of the office and sat down.

Dasha said, "I think we could both use a break. What do you have Ms. Brighton?"

Brighton smiled. "I have to say our crook is quite talented. It seems that the culprit is skilled in electronics as well as pneumatics."

Frank and Dasha swiveled their chairs in Brighton's direction.

"What baffled our security team was how someone could override the pressure sensor by preventing it from sounding during the breach. He, or she, at this point we don't know who, was able to tap into the system and equalize the pressure at both ends of the break. It is assumed that when the capsule entered the trap zone, it became imprisoned. The bypass pressure jumper served to equalize the load, thus avoiding setting off any alarms. Quite ingenious, I would say."

"I agree," Dasha said. "What about the security cameras."

"Nothing. All power leads to them were cut. But we do have our forensics team working on all possible entry and egress points. Clever or not, we'll get that SOB I'll stake my job on that."

CHAPTER 14

Marcie's naked body curled around Joe, a.k.a., Gary. As she began to wake, her body stiffened. She rolled over and swept her tousled auburn hair back away from her face. She looked at Joe as he started to stir. Both greeted each other with warm smiles.

"Sleep well?" she asked.

Joe turned on his side. "The best," he said then leaned over to kiss her lightly on the lips. He drew back, transfixed on her mischievous grin.

"Me, too," she said. "I hope this won't be the last time we see each other?"

"What about *The Company* and its rules."

"No matter. Damn *The Company* and their stupid rules."

Joe pulled her closer.

***

"When will I see you again?" Marcie asked.

"I have your number."

She appeared irritated. "That's not an answer."

Joe hadn't given that much thought. "When do you want to get together?"

"I'd say tomorrow, but I think in a couple of days would be more practical. After all, I have some private matters that need my attention." She approached Joe and gave him a kiss.

"Okay, in a couple of days I'll give you a call."

Joe opened the kitchen door.

Marcie gave a final wave before descending the stairs.

Surveying the kitchen, he remembered his uniform and pen. He reached into the shirt pocket and instantly felt it empty. Frantic at the possibility that he may have lost it, he began to feverishly search his apartment. Every crack and crevice received close scrutiny. After his futile hunt, he thought of his car, but that, too, came up empty.

Damn it, you're not thinking straight, Joe. It has to be ... somewhere ... unless ...

CHAPTER 15

Samantha Brighton, Dasha Kozar, and Frank Fitzsimons huddled around a computer monitor. Samantha pointed to a shadowy figure on the screen. "This feed came from a camera he wasn't able to neutralize. Unfortunately, that's the best picture we have of our thief. Apparently a man, but beyond that, we know nothing about him. He used some sort of a face mask to distort his image, so we can't use our face-recognition program. He looks well-built. Perhaps he works out in one of the segregated men's gym."

"Without any detail, it would be almost impossible getting a lead based on his build," Dasha countered. "We would need more information before we could canvas the immediate area. We need—"

Samantha cut her short. "This matter needs to be purged from the news. It was a colossal mistake to broadcast the break-in. The person who leaked it to the press is no longer an employee of *The Company*." She looked at Dasha and Frank. "It's fortunate you two arrived when you did. I need your expertise. That'll be your job— rewrite history and make it go away."

Frank judged from Samantha's reaction that she was trying to reassert her authority. Instinctively, he attempted to defuse the tension. "Ms. Brighton, what is the *Brahe Project*?"

She gave him a sideways glance. "That's an internal matter and doesn't concern you."

Dasha chimed in. "I distinctly heard from one of your employees, besides the lottery records, the *Brahe Project* being among the files that were compromised. Shouldn't we know more about what we are looking for?"

"When we locate the criminal who stole the lottery records we'll get those records, too."

A member of Brighton's staff entered the room. "Excuse me, Ms. Brighton, our team discovered something unusual."

"What!" she snapped.

"The log records show you signed into your account again at 20:05. Yet, the exit log indicates you left the building at 17:08."

Clearly agitated, she barked, "What terminal was used?"

He pointed. "That one—terminal three."

Brighton aimed an accusatory glance at Frank. "When did you leave last night?"

Dasha intercepted the inferred blame. "*We* left around 19:00."

Brighton abruptly stood up. "Come to my office, we'll get to the bottom of this."

***

Frank and Dasha looked on as Samantha Brighton rapidly scanned the security video. Reaching the point her cloned access card was initially used, she froze the frame. "We'll start from here."

"I see he darkened the inside windows to cover his actions," Dasha said. "He obviously didn't want to alert the night security team who monitors this floor."

A smile of victory slowly spread over Brighton's face. "I got you, you bastard." She reversed the footage to the point where the interloper entered the office. "We have our man," she called out.

"That's the same guy we ran into as we were leaving last night," Dasha said. "It was a brief encounter, but that's the man."

Frank agreed. "Yeah, I recognize that face, too."

"He evidently gained access to the building using some type of deceptive means. All we have to do is follow his movements throughout his shift," Brighton said. "We'll also question the night supervisor. I'll have the CAS agents bring her in for questioning."

"I don't think that's such a good idea," Dasha said.

Brighton gave her a probing scowl. "Why not?"

"Right now, if we involve too many people, we may inadvertently tip off all of the confederates. Think about it, your system gets broken into. The next day, your access ID is compromised by an individual who risked his life at the enterprise. An operation of this magnitude would suggest more accomplices."

"I see your point, but we're fighting against time."

Dasha nodded. "I understand, but we cannot overreact and let the culprits know, we know, that your system was hacked. Remember, it happened by chance that one of your people saw your card being used and brought it to your attention. By the way, I'm curious, what information was retrieved from that terminal?"

"My IT people told me that all the codes from yesterday were downloaded. With that data and the pilfered capsule, the information from that cylinder can be decrypted."

41

"I heard a member of your staff say it contained this month's lottery ledger," Frank said. "Other than identifying some winners, I don't see what all the concern is all about, except for the safety of the big winner."

Brighton twisted away from the monitor, glanced at Dasha and then turned her attention to Frank. "You're the literary agent—right now I want this story purged from the news. You have my permission to use every resource available—the Counterintelligence Division, the Cyber Division, the Laboratory Division, and even the Missing Persons Division. If you have to, make something up. I want this gone! Ms. Kozar and I will study the video. If we need your assistance, we'll call you. You're dismissed."

Frank looked at Dasha for moral support but found her expression one of non-involvement as she turned away toward the monitor.

CHAPTER 16

Joe was safely concealed in his hideaway when his auxiliary phone pinged with a call. He knew it could be from only one person.

Marcie's warm and enticing voice greeted him. "Hi Gary … what have you been up to?"

Joe's natural instinct for caution kicked in. *What about those 'private matters' you needed to take care of?* "Are you at work?"

"No. I didn't tell you, but I work three days on and two off."

"Sounds nice."

"I know it's late, but would you be interested in coming to my place tonight?"

Joe, shrouded in the persona of Gary, could not conceal his eagerness. "I'd like that very much. Where do you live?"

"It's a long way from your apartment. I'll make it worth your while and promise you a lovely evening." When Marcie gave the address, he was surprised at the closeness to his true sanctuary.

Having exhausted all possible places where the memory stick could have disappeared to, Marcie remained the only suspect for its loss. *She said she was going to be busy, now she is inviting me to her place on short notice. Maybe the CAS agents raided my other spot and found that I wasn't there.* Joe laughed out loud before considering the next possibility. *Their next step: use sex, to tempt me into a trap.*

Joe went to a control panel and remotely accessed his decoy apartment. All four cameras revealed that everything was the same— just as he left it earlier. Joe's survival instincts never failed him in the past. Meticulous in planning and execution, he didn't want his carnal desire to impede his judgment. Yet, he felt an intense connection with Marcie, enough so, to take a chance.

Abandoning the more casual attire he sported earlier, he selected a pair of slacks and matching jacket, dress shirt, and laid them on his bed. He went into his wall-safe and pulled out a .38 snub-nose revolver and placed it next to his clothing. He then headed for the shower.

***

Marcie's apartment building was a typical medium-echelon structure, ultra-modern, designed for functionality rather than creative design.

The red glow from an indicator over the main entry confirmed the security camera was active. Joe selected Marcie's number. Her face appeared on the monitor above the console. She gave him a welcoming gesture while the lock unbolted with a hum.

As he walked down the long hallway, two men were closing in on him from the opposite end. They were similarly dressed, almost uniform-like. Joe's first impulse was to turnaround, but their stride was so quick that given the tight quarters, there would have been a collision. Joe felt the heft of his gun against the pounding of his heart. His hands became moist, and he wondered how quickly he could draw the gun from his inside coat pocket.

Joe was partly relieved to see both men ease back and allow Joe to pass between them without incident. He forced himself not to turn around for fear of tipping his hand that he was up to some nefarious deed. The hairs on the back of his neck stiffened as he expected to be grabbed from behind at any moment. Joe slid his hand into his jacket and rested it on the gun's grip. Hearing the men's fading footsteps caused Joe to relax and continue toward the elevator.

Inside the private elevator, Joe was whisked to the fourth floor, where he found Marcie seductively leaning within her open door frame. The warm glow from the inside of her apartment accentuated her curvaceous body.

"I like your choice of clothing," Marcie said as she gave Joe, a.k.a. Gary, the once-over.

"It's nothing much," he said lightheartedly. Frozen in place, he admired her outfit. Dressed in thigh-high, open-laced purple boots with tall stiletto heels that terminated above the knees, her pink translucent pull-over blouse barely covered her nicely shaped rear. "I see you changed the color of your hair to match your boots."

She laughed. "I didn't invite you here to discuss fashion. Come." She headed into her apartment and gestured toward a sizeable curved couch. "Make yourself comfortable. Scotch?"

"Yeah, on the rocks." Joe slipped off his shoes and settled into the center of the sofa. The interior, illuminated by the light from several flickering candles, suggested either he was going to be seduced or become a victim of a cunning trap. From his position, he carefully observed Marcie preparing the drinks over a hide-a-way bar. He pondered if, at some point, she intended to slip something special to his glass. When she appeared finished he again studied the interior and was struck by the opulence afforded to a mid-level government employee. "You have done well for yourself."

"Don't let my position fool you," she said while pouring the drinks. "I get perks. Although, I think the bonuses are meant to keep me quiet after being passed over so many times."

Joe's attention drifted toward a large bookcase, set deep into a wall. "I see you have pre-alliance literature. You don't find that somewhat dangerous."

Holding two drinks, Marcie moved into the living area. "I love reading the classics on real paper-bound books. I like the smell and texture. You can't get that with a hologram." She handed a glass to Joe, then sat adjacent to him. She invitingly leaned against him.

"Do you like reading?" she asked.

"Yeah, I do."

"Funny, I didn't see any books at your place."

"I ... ah ... keep them hidden. You didn't see my other closet. Besides, I think it's best to have them out of public view." He motioned toward the bookcase. "You, of all people, must be aware that the government frowns upon having a private library."

"No matter. Victoria, close the bookcase." An overlapping panel began to blanket the books. "See, no more."

"Ingenious, but how did you get that work done without permits?"

Marcie ignored the question, took a sip of her drink, then set the glass down on the low coffee table in front of them. She reached behind the couch and produced Joe's misplaced pen.

Surprised, Joe instinctively reached out to grab it.

Smiling at his attempt, Marcie impishly pulled it away from his grasp. "Because you were so fond of this pen, I wanted to surprise you and find a replacement cartridge." She teased him by twirling it between her fingers. She then pressed down on the push button, and the tip of the pen was promptly exposed.

Joe couldn't avoid the tell as his jaw fell slightly.

Marcie again reached into a niche set into the wall behind the couch and puckishly held out a memory stick. "Yours ?" she asked playfully.

CHAPTER 17

Although Dasha offered Frank the front passenger side of the car, he declined, preferring to sulk in the backseat.

"You have to understand, Frank, I'm your friend, but sometimes I have to play the game."

"I may have lost some of my memory from the past, but I haven't lost my sense of self-respect. You left me out to dry. I felt like a damn fool when Brighton said, 'If we need your assistance, we'll call you. You're dismissed.'" Frank turned away and looked coldly out the side window as the rectilinear buildings whizzed past his view. "What am I, some trained seal who can thread a few sentences together on command?"

An icy silence blocked any challenge to his claim.

Several minutes passed before Dasha tried to repair the perceived slight. "Brighton is powerful. She has many friends. Although I outrank her on a social scale, she is the queen bee in her domain. Please, Frank, play along, for both our sakes."

Frank looked forward. "How long do we have to jump to her tune?"

Dasha let the auto-pilot take over. She turned around and met Frank's sullen eyes. "I think once this incursion and theft business is over, she'll be in a better mood. Whaddaya say, Frank, are we a team?"

Frank's somber mood began to fade. "Okay, I'll play along for a while, but there's something about my nature that tells me I can only be pushed so far." He resumed his quiet review of the moving panorama.

The car began to slow. Dasha turned and smiled at Frank. "Dinner? My treat."

Frank did not return the smile. "I'll choose something from my auto-serve machine."

When the car stopped at its bay, Frank exited first. Determined to put distance between him and Dasha he made a quick retreat toward the elevator.

"Are you sure you won't take me up on my offer?" she called out.

Without looking back, he said, "I'm sure."

47

He punched the call button and entered the elevator before Dasha could catch up.

***

Once inside his apartment, Frank isolated himself within a blanket of separation from the outside world by ordering Victoria to close all window shields. Now dark, except for the glow from various electronic devices, he shed his shoes, moved toward the bar, and ordered a brandy. He picked it up, swirled the drink and sniffed it before taking a sip. Frank felt the silence unnerving.

"Victoria, play light classical music," Frank ordered before sitting lengthwise on the couch. The melody of Pachelbel's Canon soon wafted throughout his apartment. He felt his muscles relax. He took another sip of brandy, set the glass next to him, on the floor, and crossed his arms over his chest. He stared at the pallid ceiling and wrestled with the concept of a new soul.

That's what I have done. I willingly sold my soul, not to the devil, although I may just as well have. No, I sold my soul to the State and got a new one. For what? I don't know. Freedom? Perhaps, but at what cost?

When the melody ran its course, Frank abruptly called out, "Victoria, turn off the music and turn on the television."

The screen supplanted the darkness with an ethereal glow. A female commentator stood on the top level of a short, spiral acrylic, staircase. Dressed in a blue sequined leotard, she held a hologram board using it to control the news update display.

Adding commentary to a blazing inferno which backlit her, she said, "And now for the national news. Fire crews have begun to control nearly thirty percent of the massive Hollywood fire. Originating near Mulholland Drive and Interstate 405, when a gas tanker truck exploded, it's believed to be caused by a terrorist attack. Although, at this time, no particular group has taken credit."

The camera did a tight shot of the announcer. "After that disturbing news," she began, "I am pleased to announce the report of a security breach at the Central Consortium's headquarters turned out to be a hoax. The agency announced earlier today, 'Rumors of a break-in were nothing more than propaganda spread by a dissident group.' The spokeswoman for the agency said the claim was made to discredit the outstanding job the agency does each day to keep us safe."

"That lie is my doing, and I'm not proud of it," Frank said to the screen before giving the command to shut off the television. He reached for his glass and downed its contents before retiring for the night.

CHAPTER 18

Joe was at a loss for words. Marcie's brazenness caught him off-guard, and he wondered what was next. Instinctively, he looked around, expecting any moment to be attacked by CAS agents. This was an unusual position for him to be in—he was generally in total control of the situation.

"Don't look so worried, Gary ... if that's your real name," Marcie teased. "I was just as shocked when this memory stick fell out of your pen. I intended to surprise you with a new cartridge, but it turns out I'm more surprised."

No agents swooped down on him. It seemed like a fight or flight moment. He hesitated. "What are you going to do?" he asked.

Marcie's already amused countenance erupted into a belly laugh. She struggled to contain herself long enough to say, "No matter—nothing."

"Nothing?"

"Yes, nothing. I've wanted to get back at the system for years. Right now, I don't know what this is all about," Marcie said, waving the memory stick again at Joe, "but I have a hunch it's against the law." She squirreled it again into the niche behind the couch. "What's your real name, *Gary*?"

Still, in a state of disbelief, he uttered, "Joe."

"Well, Joe, you're in for the ride of your life." Marcie leaned forward to kiss him while guiding his hand under her sheer blouse.

***

Joe lay on his back, staring up at the ceiling. Marcie lay with her supple naked breasts pressed against his chest while he gently stroked her hair. "Now what?" he asked.

"That is a good question, isn't it." Her answer—more reflective than a solution. "I'm assuming whatever is on that memory stick is pretty sensitive stuff."

"It's yesterday's code."

Marcie raised her head and shrieked, "You're the one! You're the one who broke into the tube." She shifted slightly away from Joe. "Are you a terrorist?"

Joe smiled at her outburst. "Nah, nothing like that. You could say I'm more of a ... private mercenary."

"Ahh, a soldier of fortune," she said and rested once more on Joe's chest. "How exciting. You must have many interesting stories to tell."

"Speaking of stories, you may need to have one if you are ever questioned about me."

"Why do you think I need a story? None of the alarms went off when we working last night."

Joe rubbed Marcie's back. "I was careful to hide my actions from the security cameras. But because they are, undoubtedly, checking all their log files, they'll see that someone accessed the system after normal hours."

"This is exciting," Marcie cried.

Joe looked at her with keen interest. "You are the most unusual woman that I have ever met. I'm happy to hear that you find this exciting, but there is definitely an element of risk in even knowing me. I want to be clear, this is not a game. I can walk out of your life right now, and you'll be able to plead ignorance if you're interrogated."

Marcie cuddled closer to Joe. "I've been passed over so many times for positions that I'm only too happy to pay back the system. No, Joe, you can consider us a team from now on."

CHAPTER 19

Frank wasn't in a talkative mood on the way to the office, despite Dasha's coaxings. Other than a few grunts and an occasional terse reply, his focus remained on yesterday's humiliating treatment at the hands of Brighton.

As they made their way through the atrium, Dasha halted and faced Frank. "Listen, Frank, you're going to make this whole situation more difficult if you continue with this attitude."

"I thought you were going to be more of a guardian."

She frowned and crossed her arms. "You just don't get it. We can't come into this agency and act like gangbusters, we have to gradually fit in. Like I said yesterday, work with me. Remember you agreed to that."

"You're right, I did agree. When we get to our floor, I'll act professional and do my job. About us, the jury is still out." Frank abruptly turned and began walking away.

Dasha's mobile phone buzzed in her ear. She looked at the wrist screen. "Frank wait up," she called out. "Brighton wants us to come directly to her office."

Like their shared elevator companions, who blankly eyed the digital readout of the assent, Frank and Dasha remained silent. When Frank stepped into the foyer, he became a veritable socialite with his gregarious behavior. He acknowledged the attendant, at the front desk, with an unusual familiarity that caused Dasha to give Frank a surprised sideways glance. "How's it going, Jack?" Frank greeted. "You're looking good this morning. Be a pal and tell Ms. Brighton that we have arrived and are heading to her office."

The office assistant, his mouth agape, appeared just as stunned by Frank's behavior and halted what he was doing.

Out of earshot, Frank said to Dasha, under his breath, "See, I can play the game."

With a cocky attitude, Frank strolled into Brighton's office, and without an invitation, sat down in a chair across from her desk. Dasha followed suit, but with less brashness.

Brighton gave them an inquisitive glance. "I trust you both had a good night's rest because we have a busy day ahead of us. First, our IT people have compressed all the footage of our mysterious interloper as he went about his cleaning job on this floor. Then it occurred to me that we didn't check his movements while he was at lunch."

Brighton turned toward the television behind her and pushed a button on her remote. "You'll find this interesting," she said as the screen came alive. She pointed to the freezeframe. "The supervisor's name is Marcie Reynolds. As you must already know, for security reasons, the cameras only record the action in the common areas. The reason behind that is it risks unintentional recording of sensitive material. Anyway, I noticed that she spent some time with our unknown person in one of the offices. Although, that in itself is not unusual."

She turned and faced Dasha and Frank. "What is interesting is the apparent exchange between the two of them in the cafeteria." Twisting back toward the screen, she did a fast-forward of the video. "Now, watch this."

As the action played out, it was apparent there was some physical attraction between the two of them. "Notice how Ms. Reynolds playfully pulls that pen out of that guy's pocket. We don't have audio, so we can only surmise what she may be giving him. Some personal information—a mobile phone number, perhaps?"

"Did security ever do a match on that guy's face?" Dasha asked.

"Yes, but it turned out to be a dead end. His name is Gary Duprey, and as far as our records show, he's nonexistent. That, by itself, is suspicious. Right now we're doing a blanket scan of all videotapes involving theft or robberies, hoping to piece together a dossier on him. But that takes time, and besides, he may have used anti-face recognition technology to thwart detection."

Frank lifted his right hand. "Is anyone going to protect the person who won the lottery from a possible robbery?"

Samantha Brighton shot Frank an irritated look. "What's with you and the lottery? We're trying to find the person who broke into the system."

"Hear me out," he said. "You're trying to find the identity of the person who stole the records. Okay, I understand that, but perhaps you should be more concerned with the safety of the winner. After all, it seems to me that the crook will be targeting the winner. Set a trap around that person and you'll have the thief."

Dasha agreed. "Ms. Brighton, that does make sense."

"We've already thought about that. It's being taken care of. Now let's get back to this." Brighton impatiently gestured toward the screen. "I don't want to spook anyone, especially if Ms. Reynolds is part of a more extensive criminal network. For the time being, we're tracking every movement she makes, using CAS assets."

"Okay," Dasha began, "what are we going to do?"

"This is the first significant break-in this agency ever had," Brighton said. "Originally, you two were going to help this bureau filter out disruptive news that would undermine our country's stability. Unfortunately, you got caught up in this mess. For the time being, you will continue with this case, and that will be your primary mission for now. As we get more information about the whereabouts of all players, we may need your expertise in bringing those responsible to justice, without undermining public trust."

Dasha and Frank glanced at each other.

After an uneasy pause, Brighton said, "You're dismissed. Until further notice, go check your daily news feed and do some ingenious revisions. After all, that's what I understand you do best."

As they made their way to their offices, Frank said, "Thanks for taking my side on that lottery suggestion."

"It sounded like a good idea, and I didn't want you to think I wasn't on your side."

Frank smiled. "Maybe we can be friends."

CHAPTER 20

"So, what are you going to do now?" Marcie asked as she handed Joe his memory stick.

Accepting it, Joe slipped it into his pocket and put on his jacket. "I'm going back to my place and try to figure out that code, and see what secret treasures are hidden in that cylinder."

Marcie gave him a kiss. "When will I see you again?"

Frowning and shaking his head slightly, he said, "I don't know. Right now, I can't say for sure, but I'm a little worried about you. Knowing Can-American Security, my intrusion into the system is going to be discovered, and you'll be under the microscope. If they confront you, you need to be surprised at any accusation they may level at you."

"No matter, it's not the first time I've been questioned by CAS agents. I can handle myself. Except … ."

Joe studied her. "Except what?" he asked emphatically.

"I called you on my mobile phone—there's a record."

"Don't worry about that. Before they made all phones subject to registration, I amassed several burner-phones. You can consider that link dead."

Marcie chuckled. "You are a very clever fellow."

"Thanks, but there's something that's been bothering me."

"What's that?"

"As I got out on the twentieth floor, I recognized an old associate of mine. Although it was brief, I know he saw me, but he didn't seem to remember me."

"Maybe he only looked like someone you knew."

Contemplating her remark, Joe said, "No, I'm sure it was him. There's something odd about that."

"What's his name, and what's your involvement with him?

"He had connections within Can-America—important connections. I'd rather not say too much, because at this point the less you know, the better for you." Joe approached Marcie. "Gotta run. I'll be in touch, but it won't be by phone."

Marcie gave Joe another kiss. "Leave by the rear exit. I know that camera isn't working."

"What about the front camera?" Joe asked as he began to pull open the door.

"I have a private control on that one. Your arrival won't be recorded."

Joe displayed a wide grin. "We *do* make a good team, don't we?"

"I know, and I hope we can stay a team for a long time."

***

Joe, back in his posh apartment, busied himself downloading the encrypted file that contained the winners of the national lottery. As the data was being populated, he used another terminal to set up the key-code that would break the encryption. Although occupied in his treasonable act, his concentration was divided between love and the gnawing uneasiness that his onetime ally, Rodney Bells, somehow, could be plotting against him.

The screen on one of his monitors flashed completed. He copied the file onto another memory stick before placing it into the port of the computer that held the key-code. After a few commands, the data was decrypted.

Joe, perplexed by the results, stared at the findings. His first thought was he got something wrong. He double-checked the answers. It wasn't jibberish. Everything made sense—except the winners.

CHAPTER 21

Dasha asked, "Are you going to take me up on my dinner offer from yesterday?"

Frank resumed his regular position at the rear seat of the vehicle. "Considering the grueling day we had, why not," he said adding, "but, how about someplace less formal than the last spot you took me to."

Pleased by his response, she said, "I know just the place. How about Chinese?"

"As long as they serve stiff drinks."

She chuckled then activated the transport.

***

Mr. Lau's Bar and Restaurant was a retreat for the disenfranchised—a low-profile hangout that barely displayed its enterprise. Anyone not familiar with the neighborhood could have easily overlooked its red neon sign. The district, an integral section of Old Town, was always considered on the fringe of law and order. For that very reason, Lau's place was one of many watering-holes committed to patron-vendor discretion. It was also a place that CAS agents used to ferret out informants. This juxtaposition of interests worked for both sides of the law.

Frank followed Dasha into one of the side recesses that lined the interior. They pushed aside a beaded curtain and entered a secluded room with a small table centered within its limited space. They took their places opposite each other and sat on wood-planked, distressed benches. "This certainly is less formal," Frank quipped.

The waitperson laid a couple of ragged menus in front of them. "You drink?" he asked tersely.

"Two Bah-joo, Black," Dasha answered nearly as curtly as the attendant's demand.

"Bah-joo?" Frank asked after the waiter left.

"It's a unique drink, something most Westerners aren't familiar with. We'll start with one before we eat."

"I want to ask you something, and I don't mean to question your credentials."

Dasha waved a consenting hand at him.

"You said you come from an influential family, yet you act more subservient to Samantha Brighton. Why?

"I've already explained myself, Frank. I'm here to get along and not cause waves. Besides, after I'm gone, you'll still be here, and I don't want to leave you with enemies."

Frank shook his head. "No, it's not that. You're not conducting yourself as a person would if they possessed that kind of muscle."

Before she could answer, the server returned with their order.

"You're over thinking. Take a sip of your drink."

Frank picked up the small glass and sniffed its contents. "It smells … it smells … earthy. What is this stuff again," he asked, pointing his drink toward Dasha.

"It's called bah-joo and translated, means white alcohol."

He inhaled its scent again and took a cautionary sip. His face turned crimson. "Wow, this does have a bit of a kick."

"It certainly does," agreed Dasha. "That's why I suggested having only one for now. We'll place our food order and then have another or two later. You said you wanted to unwind. Bah-joo is perfect for relaxing."

***

Frank moved with uncertainty, as Dasha guided him toward the elevator. "You okay, Frank?"

"Sure, musta been that ba-joey stuff. Shoulda quit after four."

Dasha laughed. "More like six."

"I sorta lost count."

"Well, you're almost home. I'll get you tucked in for the night."

Frank put his arm around Dasha. "I'd like dat."

She appeared to encourage him by letting him touch her. When they entered the elevator, he turned toward her and kissed her. She did not ward off his advance but gently patted him on the chest. "Hey, big guy, let's get you home first."

Once they were in Frank's place, Dasha helped him off with his shoes and jacket. While leading him through his bedroom and into the bathroom, she began to help him shed more of his clothing. "Come on, let's get you into your shower."

Down to his briefs, he slurred, "Wanna … join me?"

Dasha didn't reply. She began to unbutton her blouse. Setting it onto a nearby chair, she removed her bra. Frank moved toward her, his eyes focused on her firm breasts. They embraced. Frank fumbled for the catch on her skirt. Eagerly, she assisted him and let it fall at her feet. After removing the last bit of their clothing, Dasha led him into the shower, while the soothing spray surrounded them.

Frank's tipsiness began to wane under the refreshing water, and he began to appreciate the loveliness of Dasha's body.

***

Locked in an embrace in Frank's bed, their hair still damp, Frank and Dasha gently caressed one another.

Frank said, "Maybe we should do this more often. I think I like that bah-joo."

Dasha gave him a titillating massage on his belly. "I see it likes you too—you're ready again. I'm impressed."

"I may have lost my memory of the past, but apparently my body doesn't suffer from amnesia."

"Maybe we should save that for the morning," Dasha said. "After all, we do have to get our rest."

They both laughed and snuggled closer to each other then slowly drifted into sleep.

CHAPTER 22

Joe knew he struck gold—the problem—how to cash in. After printing out the results, he proceeded to check the other memory stick. Its placement with the lottery results was a bonus, but it puzzled him. He never heard so much as a rumor, on the street or government-generated traffic, of the Brahe Project.

When he inserted the stick into a drive, he was overwhelmed by its capacity. This was something he never encountered. His computer was incapable of downloading and printing that massive amount of data at one time. He knew, if he wanted to crack that file, he would have to upgrade his system or take the data by sections. For a moment, he considered what he'd have to do without arousing scrutiny by the government. Joe was familar with procurement regulations, and knew the task would not be easy.

The security and the size of the file tell me this has to be significant. Perhaps taking small bites is my only option, for now.

Joe realized he couldn't do anything more about the processor situation. He removed the Brahe Project's memory stick from his computer then focused once more on the lottery results. What shocked him most were the winners. All winners in the million-dollar-plus categories were listed, not by name, but bank account numbers. What struck him as odd, was the fact that all the winnings went into the same account.

This is not going to be easy to crack.

His head, swimming with questions. Joe decided to go back to do an info search, hoping to find an easy solution to at least one of his concerns. He typed in the Brahe Project. His quest found nothing that would be relevant to the present. He discovered only that the name Brahe was perhaps associated with Tycho Brahe, a sixteenth-century astronomer.

Something to do with astronomy?

Beyond the historical reference, nothing more could be gleaned as a possible explanation.

That made sense. Considering the size of the file and the historic citation, it must have something to do with astrophysics. But what?

Joe collapsed back into his swivel chair and stared at the ceiling.

And what about Rodney Bells—how does he play into all this? Does it even matter? Is it a coincidence that our paths should cross? With the law of probability, there's no such thing as a coincidence.

With daylight still remaining, Joe chose to turn in early so he would be rested for the upcoming night's activities.

CHAPTER 23

Samantha Brighton shut off the wall-screen behind her. She swiveled her chair to meet the already attentive Frank and Dasha. "That's all we have, so far, on the surveillance of Marcie Reynolds."

"When did CAS agents begin shadowing her?" asked Dasha.

Brighton cleared her throat. "Damn paperwork. They started 24 hours after my submission for round-the-clock surveillance. So, other than the short delay, everything she's doing, so far, appears normal for her position."

"Ms. Brighton, what exactly is Marcie Reynolds' job?" Frank asked.

She gave him an irritated look. "She's a supervisor. A run of the mill, night supervisor," Brighton fired back then turned her focus to Dasha. "Ms. Kozar," she began, "I don't trust anyone associated with CAS. Ever since they infiltrated the political process, I think they're self-serving and corrupt."

Dasha appeared surprised. "Why are you telling us this?"

"I've given it some thought since our last meeting. This whole operation and theft may be used by the CAS to undermine my power. You know, create suspicion about my qualifications and use it as a pretext to get rid of me. Because of that, I want you two," Brighton gave Frank an inclusionary glance, "to monitor her movements."

"Okay, if we do this, won't the CAS agents get suspicious?" Dasha began. "After all, they're also assigned to that task and may see our involvement as meddling."

"I thought about that. That's why when I made the request, I informed them we were going to make a documentary on this breach. When we catch the culprits, it will be broadcast over all networks that such brazen attempts to challenge the Can-American Union will not be without severe consequences. Your involvement will keep the CAS agents on their toes."

Frank interjected, "But I already wrote the script that the breach was only a rumor. It was televised last night."

"And you'll do another rewrite," Brighton shot back. "From what I've heard about you, you're the guru on marketing. This will be a chance to prove your worth."

Frank gritted his teeth.

"When do we start?" asked Dasha,

Samantha Brighton handed Dasha a folder. She pointed. "As soon as you go out that door."

***

Back in Frank's office, Dasha and Frank began to mull over Marcie Reynolds' bio. "I see she's been passed over three times," Dasha said, pointing to a sheet she extracted from the file folder.

"Yeah," Frank said. "She seems to have a problem with taking orders."

"She's smart," said Dasha. "Look at her education, graduated with high honors from the University of Toronto. She majored in engineering—trained in engineering innovation and entrepreneurship and a minor in astrophysics."

"Impressive. How is it that she's only in maintenance supervision?"

Dasha shook her head. "It doesn't really say in this report. My guess is, she crossed some influential people, and that alone would scuttle her career. It had to be big for her to pay such a high price."

"So, she's got an attitude, and maybe revenge is part of the equation?"

"It's hard to say. It's not uncommon nowadays for smart people to get sidelined only because of family background or for political reasons. Frank, half the people out there," Dasha pointed toward the glass partition, "have got some gripe against the system … it's the way it is."

"But, revenge is undoubtedly a motivator."

"Sure, if she was making less money. Look at her income. She's doing all right. Why would someone bite the hand … you get my drift, if she's pulling in a six-figure salary?"

"Okay, how are we going to go about this? Do we take turns tailing her, or do we work in unison?"

Dasha smiled. "Frank, after last night, I'd say we'll be working together."

"Sounds okay by me, but we can't follow her twenty-four-seven."

"I think her movements will be closely monitored when she's working. If we want to check on her then, all we have to do is scan the CCTV network footage. What we want to check is what she does after hours."

Frank stared into space. His mind drifting. It was like dreaming—only wide-awake yet teetering between reality and terror. He had the notion of being followed. No, not followed, but hunted. His hands became wet with perspiration. He wanted to run.

"Frank! Frank! You okay?"

He broke free from his confabulation. "Yeah, sure … I'm all right. Just tired, I guess. We didn't get much rest last night, did we?"

"And with that in mind," Dasha said, "We'll call it an early day. We both could use some rest before we begin checking into what Marcie Reynolds does when she's not working."

CHAPTER 24

"Hi, Marcie, it's me," Joe whispered into his mobile phone.

She giggled. "You are an impulsive guy. First, you tell me to be careful and now—"

"I know … I know. Just listen. After work meet me at that place we went to."

"You mean—"

"Don't say it … just meet me there. See you later." The phone went dead.

***

Joe parked a block away from the entrance to Marcie's work and close enough for him to see her usher the night cleaning crew back into the shuttle. He saw her give the driver a farewell wave before going toward her own vehicle.

***

Marcie approached her car and reached for the handgrip. She stealthily pulled a note from its spot, cupping it into her hand before pulling the door open.

After closing the door, Marcie cautiously opened the note. "I'm following you. Don't lock your car. Leave your remote ignition key under the front seat." She crumpled the message and started the engine.

***

As Marcie pulled away, Joe noted that another vehicle came to life and began to follow her. Knowing her destination, he trailed from a discreet distance, mindful that any sign of his involvement would trigger unwanted interest. Soon another vehicle joined the convoy, prompting Joe to fall farther back. He broke off his pursuit and decided to take another route.

By the time Joe reached the warehouse, Marcie was already inside. He positioned his car at the farthest parking spot within the lot. Joe spotted the car that tailed Marcie. From his limited view, he observed a couple of individuals monitoring the door. Because of the distance, he was unable to determine who they were.

I'll have to wait them out.

From the corner of his eye, Joe spotted a man emerging from the car that had joined the slow-moving pursuit. No one else was in that automobile. He kept track of the man, watching as he passed within a few yards of the twosome. When he entered the sham entrance to Rickey's, the two people got out of their car and also followed. Joe exited his vehicle and sprinted over to Marcie's car.

After retrieving the key, he started the engine and sped out of the parking lot. He found a deserted alleyway on the backside of the building and parked. He returned to the front entrance of the warehouse and went inside. As he entered, he brushed past the guy who earlier had been tailing Marcie. The man gave him a penetrating look. Joe needed no introduction to a CAS agent, having been familiarized with their *modus operandi,* and almost uniform-like attire. He ignored the agent's scowl and moved down the long corridor. *Keep your cool and don't look back.*

His mind still focused on the CAS agent—Joe was surprised to run into Rodney Bells and the woman from the elevator encounter. They, too, appeared to be lost. Joe gave them a passing glance and continued. This time he received a hint of recognition by both of them. He knew he couldn't go into the fake office in front of Rickey's, so he maintained his pace and turned left, down another corridor. Joe leaned his back against the wall. He waited for a few seconds before peering down the passageway he just exited. The pair were engaged in conversation and too far away for him to hear. He ducked back. The sound of approaching footsteps put him on edge. He panicked and started down the hallway, checking doors along the way for entry. Finding the janitor's closet unlocked, he entered and closed the door—it smelled of sour mops and Pine-Sol. The room was spacious for a utility room, and the presence of a cot told Joe it doubled as a hideaway spot for someone to take a nap. He quietly engaged the deadbolt and waited.

CHAPTER 25

"She's on the move," Dasha said as she engaged the car's engine. "We'll follow at a distance."

"After a day of work, she'll go home."

"Frank, she works third shift. What do you want to do after a day's work?"

"Have a drink and relax."

"Yeah, exactly. Ms. Marcie Reynolds is going to some bar to do just that."

"And according to the CAS report from a tapped phone conversation, she plans on meeting someone," Frank said glancing at Dasha. "You keep looking into your rearview mirror. You see something?"

"Someone else is following us. My guess it a CAS agent assigned to this case."

"Is that going to be a problem?" asked Frank.

Dasha laughed. "It's always a problem when they get involved. They stick out like a red and white zebra in the middle of the Serengeti." She looked up at the mirror again. "Another vehicle is shadowing us."

"Who could that be?"

Dasha didn't respond. Instead, she remained focused on the traffic behind them. "No. I was mistaken. It's pulling away."

They sat in silence for most of the trip until Marcie Reynolds made a turn into a warehouse parking lot. "A pretty busy place by the number of cars parked here," Dasha said as she slowed her own vehicle and found a spot to park.

Frank said, "I don't see any bars around here."

"We'll have to sit this one out for a while. Maybe she's picking someone up. I don't want to frighten her off. We need to know who may be working with her."

"This place seems to be a magnet for some type of clandestine activity," Frank said, waving a hand toward the building. "Notice that since we've been here, a least ten people have gone through that door. She's been in there at least fifteen minutes. Don't you think we should check on her?"

"Okay, let's go, but be prepared to make a quick exit if she starts to come out."

Frank opened the heavy warehouse door for Dasha and then followed after her. "This place smells of dust and old wood."

"Yeah, a very curious place to come to after work, don't you agree, Frank?"

"Curious indeed." The corridors were empty and no sign of activity. "Maybe we should have followed the last person in here to see where they were going?"

Dasha nodded and began to move farther down the hallway. "Let's see if we can spot anything of interest."

They came to a door that had a semitransparent window. The wording on the glass said it was a business called the International Exporters Corporation. Dasha turned the doorknob and entered. A man sat at a desk, and behind him was an old-fashioned switchboard that appeared to be more decorative than functional.

"May I help you? The man asked.

Dasha spoke up. "Yes, we're looking for a friend of ours. She's about five eight and her hair—"

The man cut her short. "I'm the only person working here, and no one has been through that door today."

"Okay … sorry to have troubled you," Dasha said and backed out of the office.

"Well, I'm at a loss. I don't know what to do next."

Frank said, "We obviously lost her. Maybe we should go back to the parking lot and stakeout her car. She's bound to come back for it."

"Sure, I guess we have no choice." Dasha turned, and Frank followed. As they proceeded toward the exit, they spotted a man coming toward them.

Dasha whispered to Frank, "Maybe this guy will lead us to where all the action is?"

As they passed him, Frank recognized the man from his office building. It was the same person he nearly bumped into as he and Dasha were entering the elevator and the focus of attention on the security tapes. He glanced at Dasha and caught the same glint of recognition in her eyes. They stopped, glanced over their shoulders, and observed the man cut into a side passageway.

"You recognized him, too," Dasha said, stopping in mid-stride and turning toward Frank. "This is no coincidence for him to be here at this time. Come on, let's follow him."

68

When they turned the corner, they found the passageway empty. Dasha and Frank moved toward a fire escape exit, trying the few doors that lined the hallway.

Frank looked at the fire escape door. "If he went out this way the alarm would have sounded. He must have escaped through one of those doors, " he said pointing down the corridor.

Dasha nodded. "These old warehouses have a maze of passages. Let's go back to the parking lot and wait for Marcie Reynolds to return to her car."

CHAPTER 26

Joe found Marcie sitting on a bar stool, her legs crossed, swinging one foot impatiently while nursing a drink.

"Well, it sure took you long enough. What was the holdup?" she asked with a hint of irritation.

The bartender approached them.

Joe held up a hand. "Scotch … neat." He turned his attention back to Marcie. "You're being followed, and I'm guessing CAS is also involved."

"No matter, there isn't any connection to me."

"You are a remarkable woman. I must say, you are pretty calm about this whole business."

The bartender set a drink in front of Joe, and he downed it. "Another, please," Joe said demandingly.

"Why did you want me to leave my remote starter under the car seat?"

Joe slid his hand across the bar and touched Marcie's hand. "First, the reason for our meeting is that I wanted to see you again."

"I have to say, you are motivated," Marcie said as her other hand stroked the back of his. "Okay, but what about the key?"

Joe, his right hand still in a hand embrace, knocked back another swig of his drink with his left hand. "Second, I suspected you'd be followed. You were … by a couple of Central Consortium employees and a CAS agent. I brushed past all of them as I made my way through the corridors. Anyway, I moved your car to the backside of this building. I'm assuming Rickey's has a back door?"

"Yeah."

"When they return to the parking lot they'll think you've left."

With a flirtatious smile, Marcie said, "And back to reason one?"

"I'll take you to my place, and I'll help you off with that uniform."

"Don't take this as an offense, but your place lacks … you know … well, um …"

"Class?"

"Yes!" she chortled.

"Well, then, I'll take you to my real place."

"You, too, are remarkable. Now, let's find that back door," Marcie said impatiently

**

Joe noted Marcie's amazement as she studied the surroundings while exiting the elevator. "Not what I'd call a penthouse suite."

Joe made a sweeping gesture. "This is the mechanical floor, it houses the electrical substations, water tanks, and pumps, along with the air handlers." Pointing down a passageway bordered with insulated pipes and electrical conduit, he said, "This is the way to my place."

"It's pretty warm in here."

"It varies a little, depending on the season, but for the most part it's regulated."

Joe ushered Marcie past several holding tanks until they came to what appeared to be a dead end. "So, is this the time you say hocus-pocus and the wall opens?" Marcie mocked.

"As you wish, milady." Joe covertly pushed a control button from the inside of his jacket. "Open sesame," he said with an incantatory flair. The wall panel began to recede and left an opening large enough to accommodate the passage of at least two people walking abreast. After it was fully open, tracks that the wall traveled on were visible on the floor.

"I thought I was ingenious with my hidden bookcase, but you have outdone me on this one."

Joe waved a welcoming hand. "Come on in."

Marcie laughed. "Said the spider … "

He urged her on. "C'mon, I won't bite."

"Now, I'm disappointed."

Once inside, the wall inched its way back into position. Joe led Marcie down a short hall that opened into a kitchen area.

Marcie let out a cry of admiration. "Wow! How did you do all of this?

"When this building was being erected, I became part of the construction crew. I saw this as an opportunity to escape from the system and still live right under their noses."

"But how?"

"During construction, I began to isolate my intended living quarters from the rest of the floor. Sometimes I would work on my own time building false partitions and reworking the power supply and plumbing. Between shifts, suddenly, walls would be in place that didn't exist on the prior shift. No one questioned it. It's a big floor."

"Okay, but what about the building inspector? He had the blueprints and could see the dimensions didn't match."

"True, but if that inspector happens to be your brother … "

"You have a brother?"

Joe frowned and moved toward the refrigerator. Not turning to address Marcie directly, he said, "Had a brother. I had a brother."

Marcie drew closer to Joe. "What happened to him?" Marcie asked in a caring tone.

"Killed—killed by a son-of-a-bitch CAS agent."

The stillness that followed hung painfully in the air. Joe cleared his throat. "Ever since then, I've devoted my life to avenging my brother's death."

Marcie's happy-go-lucky attitude melted. She opened her arms slowly like a flower, and Joe welcomed her embrace. "I'm truly sorry for your loss. How did it happen?"

What seemed like a long time neither of them spoke. Finally, Joe eased back and turned away.

Joe went to the refrigerator and opened its door. Distracted for the moment, he stared vacantly into the interior, searching for a response more than for something inside. "I'll tell you some other time. You care for a drink?" he asked mechanically.

"I think I'll have a Molson beer if you got one," Marcie said with a hint of sadness in her tone.

"Yeah, me too." Joe brought out two bottles and placed them on the island counter. After twisting off the caps, he asked, "Want a glass?"

"Nope, this is fine," Marcie said while reaching for the beer. "I'm actually surprised you had this brand." She tapped the neck of Joe's bottle with hers in a toast then took a swig.

Joe slowly came out of his pensive mood. "Some years back, I acquired a taste for this stuff. C'mon, I'll show you the rest of the place.

"A cold Molson and a tour … lead on."

CHAPTER 27

"Her car's gone. How the hell did she give us the slip?" Frank shouted.

Dasha shook her head. "Maybe when we went into that side passageway chasing that other guy, she snuck past us. We're not going to get any answers standing here in this parking lot. Let's check out her place before calling it a day."

"I'm not a cloak-and-dagger guy ... I'm an editor," Frank moaned, as they walked toward their vehicle.

"All is not lost. Remember, Marcie Reynolds is also being tailed by a CAS team. When we check in with Samantha Brighton, she'll tell us what they learned. After all, she couldn't have disappeared into thin air."

"I don't know. I think we've been outsmarted," Frank muttered as he slid into the passenger side of the car.

"Don't beat yourself up, Frank. This is only day one. She can't keep her movements secret forever." Dasha turned on the engine and sped out of the parking lot.

***

"Okay, she's not home," Dasha said while resuming her place behind the steering wheel.

Frank said, "I have a thought."

"Let's hear it."

"We have underestimated Reynolds. I think everyone involved thought all we had to do was tail her and see if she's somehow involved in the theft of that canister. Well, we know how that went, don't we."

Dasha looked at him impatiently. "I'm waiting for your suggestion."

"I'm as upset as you are. Hear me out. Let's go back to the office and get a tracking device. We can stick it on Reynolds' vehicle and be able to trace every mile. When she develops a regular pattern, we'll check out the spots she frequents."

Dasha's face lit up. "Frank, that sounds like a great idea. It'll be like following a trail of breadcrumbs." She engaged the engine of the car and slowly drove down the side street until it converged with the main artery.

Frank leaned back, reclined his seat slightly, and closed his eyes.

"Tired?"

With his eyes closed, Frank kept his meditative posture and spoke languidly into the air. "Maybe more bored than tired. This game of cat and mouse doesn't have the excitement that I thought it would have."

"Would you rather be shot at?"

Frank cast her a surprised look, viewing her comment as silly. "Watching someone is like being a voyeur—I find it a bit disconcerting." He turned back and resumed blocking out the world with fused eyelids.

"Go ahead, lay back, and relax, Frank. Take a nap if you like."

The noise-canceling acoustics of their vehicle lulled Frank into a twilight slumber before he succumbed to deep sleep. He began to dream of being surrounded by technicians or doctors. They all were wearing face masks while they kept sticking him with long probes. The prods looked more like cuesticks. Some of the rods began to bend and transform themselves into snakes. He woke with a start and gasped for air.

"You okay?" Dasha asked.

Frank bolted upright. "How long was I sleeping?"

"Not long at all, but you did zonk out pretty quickly."

Frank pulled out a handkerchief and wiped the perspiration from his forehead.

Dasha pressed, "Are you sure you're all right?"

"Yeah, yeah … sure," he said flippantly, then passively watched as their car slowly became engulfed in the darkness of the underground tunnel that led to the Central Consortium's headquarters.

The dim lights brightened again within the parking structure as Dasha guided the vehicle into her designated spot. She shut off the engine and turned toward Frank. "It doesn't take the two of us to get that tracker. Stay here and finish your nap. I'll get it myself and tell Brighton what's happening." She leaned over and kissed Frank.

Dasha's kiss was warm and intense and not only passionate but also irresistible. Like a whirling vortex, he felt helplessly drawn under her control. She held sway over him, and he felt defenseless. He both liked and hated it.

"I'll be back in no time," Dasha said. "When we get done here, I know just the thing that will make you relax." She leaned over again and gave him a quick peck on the lips and left.

***

Samantha Brighton sat behind her desk and handed Dasha the GPS tracking device. "Honestly, I didn't think we would need this. I thought it would be an easy assignment to see if she's working with someone."

"What about that CAS team?" Dasha asked.

"Team my ass. There's only one person assigned to each shift. Personally, I still think they're more interested in me than Reynolds. That agent you saw tailing her … filed a report that she simply gave him the slip. That's it … gave him the slip. What the hell does he expect her to do, draw him a map of where she's going? Idiots!"

Dasha grinned at Brighton's outburst.

"What about Frank?"

"What do you mean?" Dasha asked.

"Did you sleep with him yet?"

Dasha steepled her fingers. Leaning back smugly, she let loose a gratifying sigh. "Yes," she breathed as her face lit up with delight.

"Good," Brighton said weakly.

CHAPTER 28

Marcie studied the computer screen. "Wow! Do you understand the importance of this stuff?"

Joe sat eyeing Marcie more than her monitor. "I think I do. Someone, or some group within the government, is skimming off the lottery. Every large winner shares one thing in common—the same bank account ... different names, but one bank account."

Shifting her attention from the display to Joe, she asked, "How is that possible ... I mean, the odds of that are—"

"Impossible."

Marcie's eyes widened, and a flicker of comprehension appeared to take hold. "That's right, it's impossible, but if the game was fixed ..."

Joe nodded. "The house always wins—in this case, the state. That's the second part of the equation. Because they control the winning numbers, the government selects which numbers."

"How do they do that?"

Joe eased back in his chair. "I think I know. The combination of numbers is determined by numbers not selected by any of the players. When you consider the odds of winning are one in fourteen million, it's easy to pick when the jackpot is ripe—thus large winnings."

"Do you have any idea who's doing this?"

Joe reached over and shut down his computer. "The fact that the canister was sent only to the public affairs division tells me it's someone in that department, or ..."

Marcie swiveled her chair in Joe's direction. "Or what?"

"Or, it's a Can-America operation designed to con people out of ever winning any of the significant prizes."

"Isn't it going to be tough finding out who owns that bank account?"

"That is where you come in. If it's an individual we should be able to identify the person or persons involved. It should be easy to get a list of people working on that floor. I need to tap into the personnel database." Joe began to smile. It widened to the point of nearly breaking out into laughter. He checked himself. "Every system has a weak link."

"And?" Marcie asked and appeared riled by his teasing.

"The cafeteria ... that's the weak link. Everyone eats there, and they all use their ID cards to debit their accounts."

"Okay, how do I get that information?"

"When you're working, you gain access to the mechanical room, insert a memory stick into a port, and download the day's receipts. Simple."

Marcie got up and stretched. "No matter ... I'll do it. There aren't any security cameras in that room. After all, as you said, every place has a weak link."

"Good. I'll give you a memory stick and a burner-phone before you go. We now know that CAS is tailing you, so you'll have to be extra careful. All our meetings will have to be where we control the situation. Never drive directly here. I'll always pick you up."

"Got it. Now, I've seen your place except for the bedroom. I'm assuming you have one?"

***

Joe followed Marcie out of his bedroom. She stopped, adjusted her tousled hair, and turned back to him. "I have to say my first impression of you was way off," she said, with the self-assurance of a woman who generally got her way.

"And what was that?" Joe asked smugly, aware her boastfulness was only a foil to shield her from complete submission.

She laughed. "Bookish," she answered coyly.

"Bookish?"

"Yeah, bookish." She gently ran her finger down his bare chest.

He grabbed and pulled her close. "You are a tease," he said and gave her a forceful kiss.

Submitting, at first, with equal affection, she pulled back. "Tease? You're the tease. We can't keep this up if we're ever going to get anything done, now can we?"

"You're right ... it's just that ... "

"I know. I feel the same way. It's getting late. I have to get going. Although I could use another beer."

"Sure, nothing like a gal who knows what she wants," Joe said. "I'll meet you by the computer section. I want to get my shirt first." He turned back to the bedroom before going into the kitchen. Supplied with two bottles of beer, he found Marcie eyeing a printout near the computer monitor.

"What's this all about?" she asked pointing to the stack of sheets.

"I don't exactly know," Joe said, as he handed her one of the bottles. "It has something to do with astronomy, that's all I can tell so far. It's some classified venture called the Brahe Project. I'm not too sharp on stellar stuff. How about you? Do you know about this junk?"

"I have a minor in astronomy and astrophysics from the University of Toronto—St. George Campus. I'm guessing this so-called *junk,* is more important than that stuff." She pointed to the lottery printout.

"You're welcome to have a go at it, but I think it best if you did your research over here."

Marcie smiled. "You wouldn't have any ulterior motives, would you, eh?"

"Ha," he laughed. "Remember, I'm bookish."

CHAPTER 29

Terror held Frank in place. He wanted to run, but his legs remained immobile, bound by the unseen tentacles of an evil specter. He thought he was in a room, but it wasn't a room—it was a cage. He tried to reach out to the bars in an attempt to pull himself free. The distance appeared near, yet his hands, like shadows, felt useless as they passed through the bars. People clothed in white taunted him and jabbed him with poles. They stayed on the outside of his enclosure, their stinging probes lashing at him like thousands of enraged bees. The bars melted. A large door opened, allowing a creature, who lacked definition, to enter. Frank felt its evil. He gasped.

"Frank! You all right?" Dasha asked as she opened the car door.

Wide-eyed and dazed he looked at her with alarm. "Yeah ... just a nightmare."

"Nightmare?"

"Just a stupid dream."

Dasha slid into her seat. "You want to talk about it?"

He gave her a questioning glance. "Why? It's just a dream."

She placed a small metallic box on the dashboard. "Sometimes, dreams give clues about how we are feeling. I just thought ... " Dasha pushed a button on her remote starter, and the engine came to life. "Maybe you need a rest. You didn't have much of a break after being released from—"

"You can say it ... jail."

"It wasn't that. It was more of a hospital. You know, a place to get well." She pointed to the device on top of the console. "We'll drop that off and take a break. We can get a takeaway and have a nice dinner at your place. Whadda you say, Frank?"

Frank knew he was being handled. He thought of the lovemaking and how her body willingly responded to his desire. He wanted someone to love and someone to love him in return. She had an emotional hold on him. For him, it was awkward affection, tempered with mistrust. He faced her. "I think that's a great idea."

Am I to sell my body—my soul—for sexual gratification?

Dasha maneuvered the car into the center lane and accelerated out of the parking garage.

***

By the time they reached Marcie Reynolds' place, Frank had mentally adjusted to the reality of the carnal bond that Dasha held on him. The pleasure was too great to overcome. It wasn't that he disliked her, but her charm and sexuality made it impossible for him to seek an alternative. Even without bars, he felt he was a prisoner.

Dasha eased the vehicle into an isolated area behind Marcie Reynolds' apartment building. "Here's the master control for gaining access to her garage," she said. "I'll deal with the tracker. This shouldn't take long."

"Why didn't the CAS handle this?" Frank asked.

"Because Brighton doesn't trust them, that's why," Dasha snapped. "Now, let's go."

Their movement was masked in shadows as they skirted around the islands of light that served as a defense against nighttime interlopers such as themselves. Dasha held point while Frank safeguarded the rear, looking for any sign of them being discovered.

When Dasha reached the gate, she waited for Frank to disengage the lock. He waved the card over the security device. The faint sound of a click signaled the latch was unlocked, and the two of them slipped through the partially open entrance.

Pointing, Dasha said, "I see her car. Stay here and watch the entrance while I take care of the tracker. Keep the door open a bit so we can make a quick exit."

Dasha hurried toward Reynolds' car. As she reached it, the door at the far end of the parking garage opened, and a solidarity form moved down the center aisle, toward Dasha. The figure was rapidly advancing.

Frank recognized Marcie Reynolds and made a quick decision to thwart any possible awkward confrontation or wariness on her part. He let the door close and shouted, "Brooke! Hold on and wait for me." Leaving his post, he rushed toward Dasha. "Hey, I'm sorry." He smiled and opened his arms, giving her a hug.

The look of bewilderment on Dasha's face melted into a grin. Turning away from the advancing Reynolds, she reciprocated his embrace. Frank pulled Dasha toward him while turning his back on Reynolds, who gave the couple a passing glance. Keeping their faces buried in a kiss, they waited until Reynolds opened her car door. Before she could start her car, Frank and Dasha moved toward the entry that only moments ago was used by Marcie Reynolds.

"That was a close call. She left for work earlier than I had expected," Dasha said, gently withdrawing from Frank's embrace. "Who's Brooke?"

"Just a name that popped into my head. I had to think of something fast to explain why the two of us were in the garage. I believe we just lost our advantage of anonymity. I tried to conceal our faces as much as I could, but I'm certain she would recognize us if we were to meet again."

"I don't know where she's going right now, but we'll have another chance when she gets to work. We're missing too much of her whereabouts." Waving the tracker, she said, "Come on, Frank, let's stake out the office building so we can plant this, and we'll call it a day."

***

Frank stared upward, watching the artificial projection of cirrus clouds gradually make their way across the ceiling. To his left, the wall glowed with the scene of soothing waves lapping at a pristine beach. The peaceful ambiance of the sound of the ocean and occasional cry of a distant gull enhanced the romantic mood. Dasha's head rested heavily on his chest. She was asleep, and he didn't want to wake her. He was content, or at least, thought he was. The moment remained too perfect for questioning otherwise.

CHAPTER 30

Frank Fitzsimons and Dasha Kozar watched as Samantha Brighton paced back-and-forth behind her desk. "You're telling me she hasn't made contact with anyone this past week?" she fumed.

"She finds a secluded spot to park her vehicle," Dasha began, "and mysteriously blends into either the crowd or finds an obscure building and never comes out the same way she went in. She's clever."

"I've had enough of this game of cat-and-mouse. I'm calling Marcie Reynolds in for questioning. She's not going to make fools of us anymore. Do you two want to sit in on the interrogation?"

Dasha cleared her throat. "We didn't say anything to you at the time, but she saw us during our first attempt to put the tracker on her vehicle. I don't know if she got a good look at us in the dim lighting, but I think it would be best to limit our contact with her."

Brighton regarded Frank with a contemptuous look. "Your doing?" she asked.

"No, mine," Dasha spoke up. "I was in an awkward position and would have been found out if Frank hadn't acted the way he did, at the time."

"Fine, fine. I'll put Reynolds on CCTV when I question her. You two can watch from another room. You know, study her reaction. I also think by putting pressure on her, she may get nervous, perhaps careless, and trip up. I'm tired of this. I'll give her a call to come in this afternoon. In the meantime, study those records of the stops she has been making. See if there is a common denominator of some kind, you know, a pattern—"

"Ms. Brighton," Dasha interrupted. "Can you send the interview feed to my office? I'm far enough away from your office, and it would be less likely that she would run into us there."

"Fine."

"What time," Frank asked.

"Two," Brighton snapped, then gave them a penetrating look. "Why are you waiting? Get on it."

Outside Brighton's office, Frank's anger spilled over. "She's not much for subtlety, is she?"

"Her job is on the line," Dasha replied as they walked back to her office.

Frank felt things were purposely being withheld from him. "My gut tells me it's more than that."

***

Sitting comfortably in his office, Frank thought Marcie Reynolds looked confident—too confident. Only the back of Samantha Brighton was visible. Dasha sat in the chair next to him. With their chairs tilted back, they viewed the CCTV feed from Brighton's office.

"Ms. Reynolds, do you have any idea why I called you into my office?"

Straight-faced and without any apparent uneasiness, she answered, "No."

After a moment of silence, Brighton said, "There has been a serious security breach in this office, and it occurred during one of your shifts."

"This is the first time anyone has mentioned that to me. Are you accusing me?"

"Let me show you something," Brighton said forcefully as she reached for the controls on her desk. Brighton's back glowed from the screen behind her. "She turned toward the projection and pointed, allowing Frank and Dasha to get a glimpse of her face before turning back to Reynolds. "Do you remember this man from the cafeteria?"

"Yeah. He told me his name was Gary. What of it?"

Brighton lashed out. "His full name is Gary Duprey, which is an alias. Our records show that he is the one who broke into our system and stole files while you were on duty. Do you see that picture, Ms. Reynolds?" Brighton made a jabbing gesture at the picture behind her.

"Yeah," Reynolds replied without a hint of nervousness.

Brighton's voice rose. "You two look pretty cozy—almost too cozy. Keep your eyes on the screen, Ms. Reynolds."

Frank could she Reynold's eyes dispassionately watching the recording.

Brighton also turned her chair and watched the video. She held a remote control and pointed. "Why are you reaching for that man's pen, Ms. Reynolds?" She swiveled back to face Reynolds.

Marcie Reynolds crossed her arms over her chest. "Is that what this is all about? The guy was filling in because one of my regulars called in sick. I was attracted to him. I was flirting. That's all."

"Why did you reach for his pen?"

"I planned on giving him my phone number. I intended to write it down."

"Did he call you?"

"No," Reynolds said, dropping her arms onto her lap. "I guess he was just playing me."

After a protracted silence, Samantha Brighton turned off the screen. "You may go now, Ms. Reynolds, but before you do, I want to emphasize that Gary Duprey, or whatever he calls himself, is dangerous. If he should contact you, I want you to notify me as soon as he does. Got that, Ms. Reynolds?"

Marcie Reynolds rose from her chair. "Got it."

As soon as she left, Samantha Brighton turned toward the camera behind her. "Come into my office," she ordered.

Within a few minutes, Frank and Dasha joined Brighton in her office. "She's a cool customer. I want you two to watch everything she does. That's your top priority. Mr. Fitzsimons, forget about reviewing scripts for now. You and Dasha get as close to her as you can without spooking her. After my interview, she'll try to get in touch with someone—if she's an accomplice in this, we'll nail her. No one is going to make a fool out of me." Brighton's eyes flashed. "Got that?"

Frank and Dasha rose. Dasha replied, "Yes, Ms. Brighton, we'll monitor every move she makes. You have my assurance."

***

Dasha called out to the bartender. "Two more, please," she said, signaling with her index finger that their glasses needed refilling.

Frank showed his annoyance with Dasha by staring at the giant television screen positioned over the back bar. "Don't you think we should be getting some sleep if we're going to be tailing Marcie?" he said without turning to her.

When Dasha twisted toward him, he rotated his chair to meet her gaze.

"Relax, Frank. Just because Samantha Brighton says jump, we don't necessarily have to right away. Marcie Reynolds is working ... by that I mean ... we know her movements are being watched on CCTV. If it makes you feel better, after our second drink, I'll take you home to catch some rest."

"That's sounds fine by me. And, by the way, I'm glad we walked through the atrium to the Company's bar. After talking with Ms. Brighton, I needed a quick drink, too, but I'm dog-tired and want some shuteye." He turned back to the screen.

Dasha, too, looked up and said in a surprised voice, "Well, that's interesting."

Although the volume remained low, they both were able to hear the news broadcast. A rather stout woman, dressed in an overly tight khaki safari outfit, held a slim microphone close to her overemphasized, pouting lips. "Rachel Cleaves here, broadcasting live from Madison, Wisconsin."

In the background, several CAS emergency vehicles formed a defensive perimeter around a large lump of something. The hunk, still unidentified, was shrouded in a flexible metallic covering. The newscaster glanced over her shoulder and turned back toward the camera. "I've been informed that a group of students attacked a K-5 robot and tipped it onto its side. Following Isaac Asimov's first rule of the 'Three Laws of Robotics,' the robot did not retaliate, but only called for assistance. Officials tell me that video will be retrieved from the robot's black box, and the perpetrators will be apprehended."

A slight smile formed on the announcer's face. "A spokeswoman said that these incidents of robot tipping will not go unpunished. Back to you, Perera."

Perera, dressed in a glistening violet-colored metallic body-hugging outfit, appeared amused. "And now on to the rest of today's news ..."

Frank glanced at Dasha, who seemed equally amused. "Well, you have to admit, it is funny," Frank said as he reached for his second drink.

Dasha's toughness melted. "Yea, it is," she said.

CHAPTER 31

"Where are you calling from?" Joe asked Marcie.

The sound of a running shower cascaded in the background. "From my bathroom. I'm using the phone you gave me. You don't have to worry—Victoria isn't installed in here. I was interviewed before starting my shift last night. We should talk, but not over the phone."

Joe hesitated. "You know the rest area off the Grand Parkway, near Liberty Mall?"

"Yeah."

"Meet me there in an hour. Take the south exit. Go into the women's restroom. Check to see if you are being followed. When you leave, go to the north side parking lot. I'll be there with my car running. Be prepared to hop in. Are you scared?"

Marcie let out a gush of laughter. "No matter … this is exciting. I'll be there, and I have what you wanted."

***

The Grand Parkway interchange was a vast complex and hub for several connecting thoroughfares. Marcie entered the parkway's ladies' room wearing a bright red jacket. She circumspectly checked her surroundings watching for anyone who may have tailed her. After selecting a stall, Marcie removed her coat, hung it on the door's hook, and left. She merged with the other women. Having intentionally worn nondescript clothing, she easily blended in with most of the conventional fashions that filled the restroom. Marcie followed the concourse, deliberately staying as near as possible to clusters of people.

When the opportunity presented itself, she broke free and slid into the passenger side of Joe's car. "What a rush. I can't say when I've had more fun," she said while securing her seatbelt.

Like the swiftness of Marcie's retreat, Joe pushed the accelerator and merged into the Grand Parkway traffic. "You are an amazing woman," Joe commented as he gave her an admiring look.

"You're not just saying that to get me into bed, are you?"

Joe laughed. "You have the list of employees in the Central Consortium's building?"

"Yeah, no matter, it was easy. I have it right here." Marcie patted her left breast.

Joe gave her a quick look before returning his attention back to the traffic. "You said you were interviewed. I'm assuming it concerned me?" He set the car on autopilot.

"Yeah, the director, Samantha Brighton, tried to get me to talk. I was mentally prepared for the interrogation. So, it was easy to stay focused on denial. She showed me some footage of us in the cafeteria. She tried to make a big deal about it."

"So, what did you say?"

"I said I was flirting with you, and you never called me after I gave you my mobile phone number."

"You think she bought it?"

Marcie let out an unconcerned moan. "I've seen how these bureaucrats work. No, I'm sure she didn't, and that's to our advantage. I know how they reason things out—she thinks I'll let my guard down and they'll catch me redhanded. I'm too smart for them."

"I like your moxie."

"By the way, what are you going to do with that lottery information?" Marcie asked.

Joe shook his head. "I'm not sure. I thought about tapping into their special government account and siphoning off some funds. After all, I do need capital to function."

"Won't that identify you?"

"I have several offshore accounts. Once the transfer is made, another transfer is made, and the first account is terminated. The trail ends there. Later, I'll use an alternative account for a future transfer."

Marcie nodded. "I understand, but couldn't the perpetrator or perpetrators do the same?"

"All government officials have anti-export firewalls built into the system that prevents them from engaging in international trade or collusion."

"Okay ... but what about you? Why are you able to do it?"

Joe smirked. "Because I exploit diplomatic cables."

"This whole system is dangling on a thread. Someone has to be getting pretty nervous. This could blow up and be the biggest scandal in decades. It'll send a shockwave through the system, and make it difficult for the government to survive, if not impossible."

A smile formed on Joe's face. "Yeah, I know. It's a win-win for us. When we find out who the administrator of that bank account is, we'll zero in on that person."

"And do what?"

"It all depends on who's behind it."

***

Joe and Marcie made themselves at home in Joe's retreat. Marcie went into the kitchen for a couple of beers while Joe made himself comfortable in front of his desk. When Marcie joined him, he was about to insert the memory stick into his computer. "I'll start working on the list you downloaded," he said, taking the beer from Marcie. "In the meantime, why don't you have a go of it on that Brahe Project stuff."

Marcie took a seat in front of the adjacent terminal. "I'm not certain how much work I can accomplish in three hours, but I'll give it a try. By the way, did you have any idea what you would find when you selected that day and time to steal the capsule?"

Joe pivoted his chair in Marcie's direction. "Everything was designed around the security of the area, time of night, and most importantly, the day of the month. Like any company, reports are generally done at the end of each month, but the data is usually submitted at the beginning of the next month. I just thought it the most advantageous period."

Joe pointed. "That stuff you're working on … a bonus."

"So, it was blind luck that you snagged this Brahe Project?"

"Yep, like fishing—sometimes you don't know what you'll catch. In this case, I believe I caught a trophy fish." Amused, he turned his attention back to his computer.

Marcie began printing several reports, stacking them in an orderly fashion alongside her workstation. Joe, on the other hand, watched as rows of names populated his screen. He stopped abruptly, and one name caught his interest.

CHAPTER 32

Frank fidgeted in the car. He looked at Dasha and saw her yawn before closing her eyes. "I'm afraid Marcie Renyolds has outsmarted us again," Frank said in an attempt to keep her from falling asleep. "It's been over an hour, and it's hard to say when she's coming back to get her car."

Dasha stretched in place then turned toward Frank. "Damn, if our cover wasn't blown back in her parking garage, I should have followed her into the ladies' room. It's as if she vanished into another dimension."

"Even if she does come back and we're still here, we won't have a clue where she's been," said Frank, staring blankly at the passing traffic. "Why aren't we tracking her by the signal from her mobile phone?"

"Brighton told me that the boys from CAS tried to ping her phone."

"And ... what happened?"

"She leaves her phone in her car. So, right now, her phone is telling us the exact information as the tracker."

Frank looked at Dasha, "I have an idea."

"What's that?"

"Her car has been sitting long enough. Contact the rest area security personnel. Tell them that you believe the vehicle has been abandoned. You can get authorization to have it towed."

Dasha skeptically eyed Frank. "What good will that do?"

"Think about it. When Reynolds returns, she'll have to contact the police. She may be using a burner phone, so the only option she'll have is using it. We set up a tap on the nearby tower to monitor the call."

"Go on." Dasha's face began to light up.

"We link her phone and get a GPS lock on it—"

"And then we track her every move, not just the car's," Dasha said.

"Exactly!" Frank exclaimed. "You seem to have a better rapport with Samantha Brighton. I think you should get in touch with her ASAP. After you make the call, I'll go to the security station and see about getting that car moved. I don't know how much time we have before Reynolds returns."

Dasha retrieved her phone and made the call. "It is a great idea," Dasha said over the phone to Brighton, "but I have to confess it was Frank's."

Dasha listened in silence then said, "Yes, Ms. Brighton." She terminated the call and looked at Frank. "Brighton ordered us to stay here until Marcie Reynolds returns. She wants us to follow her back to her apartment."

"Okay," Frank said. "I'll go and talk with the security attendants."

When Frank returned, Dasha said, "I hope you were listening when I gave you credit for this plan?"

"And what was Brighton's response?"

"What do you think?" Dasha hesitantly replied.

"No surprise," Frank said, visibly upset.

After passing the time in idle chatter and supervising the towing of Marcie's car, Frank and Dasha returned to their car to wait. When Marcie returned, they perked up and observed every move she made.

Marcie appeared confused as she began searching the parking lot. She systematically weaved her way through the aisles between vehicles. Seemingly giving up, Marcie reached into her purse and drew out a phone. She paused in mid-action and apparently changed her mind and returned the phone.

Dasha grabbed for her phone. "She's here," she told Brighton. "Stand by. I'll let you know if she uses another phone."

Reynolds began to walk toward the security office.

"Damn. What if she uses the security office's landline?" Dasha said.

Frank trained a set of binoculars on Reynolds as she entered the security's headquarters. "Let's not panic. When I went in there to have her vehicle towed, those guys didn't seem like the cooperative type."

Following a lengthy visit, Reynolds walked out of the office and immediately pulled out the cell phone from her purse again.

"She's going to use her phone!" Frank exclaimed.

"Ms. Brighton, she's calling someone," Dasha said.

"Keep an eye on her. I'll get that bitch yet," Brighton replied caustically.

Continuing to train his binoculars on Reynolds, Frank observed her move to a secluded side of the terminal. Following what appeared to be her first call, she dialed another number. Frank detected a shift in her demeanor. Gradually her face began to change from worry to amusement. "That's odd."

"What's odd?" Dasha asked.

"She's smiling. She has to be calling her cohort."

Dasha asked, "Do you think she's calling him for a ride?"

"Who knows. I think it's worth our while to stay here to see who picks her up."

Dasha relayed Franks' suspicion to Brighton.

"Good," Brighton replied. "We've got our GPS link. Now stay with her and see what's she's up to." Characteristically, she hung up abruptly.

"Hello?" Dasha asked, before putting down her own phone. "Brighton's not for the niceties of social norms," she muttered under her breath.

Still focused on Reynolds and her unknown associate, Frank countered with a disinterested grunt. He lowered the binoculars and looked at Dasha. "If it were me, I'd call a taxi and go to the impoundment lot to get my car." He raised the field glasses back to his eyes.

"If that's the case, Frank, we shouldn't have too long to wait."

CHAPTER 33

"I trust you, and Mr. Fitzsimons had a good night?" Samantha Brighton asked as she rummaged through some papers on her desk.

"Rested, if that's what you mean," Dasha replied tersely.

"You already told me you two are sleeping together. The point I'm making is—did you have any success in seeing what Reynolds is up to … nothing more?"

Dasha shifted nervously. "We tailed Marcie Reynolds to the impound lot, where she picked up her car. After that, she went to her apartment and presumably to bed. Frank and I waited for two hours before turning in ourselves."

"You're starting to get defensive. Don't get too attached to Mr. Fitzsimons. Remember, you have a job to do." Brighton's frown softened when she reached for a sheet of paper from the stack she assembled in front of her. "Here!" She thrust the sheet towards Dasha.

"What's this?"

"I know you two need to rest, so while you and Frank were *idle,* we were able to track her every move." Pointing, she said, "That's the address of Ms. Reynolds', we assume, her partner in crime."

Dasha's eyes widened. "That's a pretty affluent part of town and isn't that—?"

"Yes, it is … the address of *my apartment* building."

"What does that mean?"

"It *means* that she may be involved with some pretty important person or persons. I'll be honest, this also confirms my suspicion that someone in the Can-American government is out to get me. If I can find out who, I'll make sure they'll regret even trying."

"Considering the GPS in Reynolds' phone will only disclose her grid location, not altitude, how do you want me to proceed?"

"My apartment building has eighty floors with four spacious apartments on each one. I know it's a herculean task to find the one in three hundred and twenty. And because of the sensitivity, and my suspicions, I don't trust anyone, except you. Because of my position, you'll be on your own. I know you may run the risk of being identified, but I can't think of any other option. You'll have to be as inconspicuous as possible."

"What about the CAS agent assigned to this case?"

"That is a problem, isn't it?" Brighton leaned back in her chair and appeared to contemplate the situation. "I think I'll play it by ear for now. In the meantime, see what apartment she's visiting." She slammed her fist on the desk. "I want the bastard!"

"What about Frank?"

"What about him?"

"I thought my primary objective was to ferret out all of his accomplices."

"Yeah, I know, but this is more important. If Frank Fitzsimons should show any sign of remembering, or if any of his associates make contact with him, it'll be a bonus. But right now, this is more important." Brighton leaned forward on her desk. "And as long as we're on the subject, do you see any change in his behavior?"

Dasha nodded. "Yes, he told me he's been having some strange dreams."

"What kind of dreams?"

"He doesn't want to talk about them. I think it's the post brain surgery operation syndrome."

"This is the first time our department had a rehab patient. Honestly, I don't trust Frank. I'm skeptical of the entire program."

"Samantha, if I may be blunt, it shows, and I don't think it's helpful with Frank's recovery. I think you could cut him a little slack."

Brighton curled her lips and appeared deep in thought. Leaning back in her chair, she said, "Okay, I'll try. Now go find *your Frank* and see who Marcie Reynolds is visiting. In the meantime, I'll get in touch with my apartment's security team to let them know that you're on a special assignment for me. I don't want to say too much about this mission because I don't know who all is involved. At least you'll have access to the CCTV system."

***

Frank stared at the geometric cityscape, fascinated by the pulsating sunlight that played over its steel and glass exoskeleton as the sun raced between the broken clouds. His meditation was interrupted when Dasha entered his office.

"Deep in thought, Frank?" she asked.

He turned toward her. "Nothing else to do, since Brighton took me off any editorial assignments."

"Well, Frank, that's about to change. We've been assigned to tail Marcie Reynolds full time, and we now have an address where she skips off to after work."

Frank saw a smile slowly form of Dasha's face. "You have more news?" he asked.

Dasha moved to one of the side chairs and took a seat. "As a matter of fact, I do. Our elusive Reynolds is seeing someone in the very same building where Brighton lives."

"That's interesting," Frank said, then looked back at the cityscape. "Given Brighton's social status, that can only mean one thing … Reynolds may have some pretty well-heeled friends."

"That's Brighton's assumption, also."

"How many apartments are in that building?"

"Three hundred and twenty."

"Wow! Nothing like giving us a challenge." Frank moved away from the window and sat in his desk chair.

Dasha shook her head. "It sounds like more of an undertaking than it really is. We have a tracker on her phone and car. The car tracker will tell us when she's on the move. So far she's been too clever for us to see how she meets him. Instead, we'll follow the GPS signal."

"Okay, that sounds simple enough, but we can't exactly follow her that closely when she enters the building."

"Brighton said she'll call ahead to the security station and let them know we'll be needing their assistance. So, you see, it shouldn't be too difficult."

Frank felt he was on an emotional ride and wasn't sure he wanted to be a passenger anymore. "What's our next move?"

"We go back to our apartment building and get some rest. Right now, we need to be on the same sleep schedule that Marcie Reynolds is on."

CHAPTER 34

After swiping his security pass on the reader, Joe held the door for Marcie. "Knowing that you're not a registered tenant here, how do you manage to get in?" Marcie asked.

Joe pushed the call button for the elevator. "I have successfully tapped into the building's mainframe and always update the codes. It was easy. Unless someone were to do a complete rewire of the system, no one would ever notice the additional lines nicked from the electrical hub."

The doors to the elevator yawned open. "What about that?" Marcie said, giving a slight nod to the placement of an apparent camera over the control panel.

"The residents in this building objected to the presence of video monitoring in the elevator, considering it intrusive. So they can only be turned on in an emergency." Joe punched in a code before selecting his floor. He studied Marcie as she watched the numbers on display rapidly change.

Marcie asked, "How do you know they're off?"

"Anytime they're live, a red light indicator goes on. So, if anyone were actually watching this entrance to the building, they would have only seen us getting in."

"I find this mind-boggling." Marcie stepped out onto their floor. She pointed to the equipment. "Doesn't someone have to care for all this stuff?"

"Yes, but most of the checking is done remotely. If there's a problem, a technician comes here to deal with it. And once in a while, a judicious night watchman might come to inspect. I've also seen them come here to take a nap."

They began walking toward the concealed entrance. "Well, you can't be sauntering through here when that happens, eh?"

Joe pulled his control device from his jacket pocket. Waving it in the air, he said, "If someone is here this little gadget lets me know." He pressed a button on it, and the hidden panel slid open. He motioned. "You know the way. Meet me in the computer room." Joe slipped off his jacket. "I'll get us a couple of Molsons."

Marcie beamed. "Hey, what are the odds that you're a Molson lover, too?"

Smiling, he said, "Considering we're south of the forty-ninth? Infinitesimal."

When Joe found Marcie, she had already logged in on her PC. "Eager to begin, I see," he said as he placed the bottle of beer on the countertop.

Grabbing the bottle, Marcie gave Joe an air salute before taking a sip. "This whole Brahe Project is fascinating."

"Like I said, that stuff is beyond my comprehension. What's so interesting about it?"

While the computer cycled through boot-up, she turned her swivel chair in Joe's direction. "What I can make out so far, back in 2018, several space probes were launched to basically map the universe."

Joe took a large gulp of his beer, sat, and held the bottle on his lap. He ogled Marcie's exposed legs that were seductively crossed.

Catching his eye, she said, "Um ... business first."

With a look of chagrin, he said, "But of course. So, what about that probe."

"It was called the Dark Energy Spectroscopic Instrument Science Mission, or the DESI Project."

"Okay, what does *dark energy* have to do with the universe?"

Marcie chuckled. "The *universe* is mostly made of dark matter. Because it is hidden from the naked eye, special equipment needs to be used to detect its presence. So, as near as I can determine, what you have here are the results of those investigations."

"Does it have any monetary value?"

"I suppose ... to a scientist. And before you get ahead of yourself, I'm confident when this data was stolen, another report was sent to the Central Consortium. So, like your lottery information, it's only a copy. Although the lottery stuff has the potential of bringing down some powerful people. And about that, do you have any idea who's stealing that money?"

"Not until I check that list of employees you downloaded." Joe held out his hand. "Let's have a look at that now."

Marcie stood up and strolled toward Joe. Reaching into her bra, she partially exposed the memory stick in the cleft between her breasts. "Help yourself."

Joe enthusiastically reached for it, letting his hand pause within her cleavage.

She gave him a quick peck on the lips. "Remember, first work, then play." Marcie winked, pulled back, as Joe secured the memory stick.

Waving the stick in the air, he said, "It shouldn't take too long to see who's tapping into those funds."

Marcie started for her computer, paused, and turned back. "If you don't mind, I'll keep working on the Brahe material."

"Go right ahead. I think there's enough for both of us to keep busy." He took the still warm memory stick and placed it into a processor receptacle. The screen quickly populated with rows of names and corresponding numbers. Surprised and frustrated by the complexity of the display, he leaned back in his chair, contemplating his course of action. *This is not going to be as easy as I thought.*

Like with most of his undertakings, he pushed aside his misgivings and dove in. He began by isolating each repetitive group by its frequency, assuming the more permanent staff would appear more regularly. After collecting his data, he segregated them numerically. Only the last four numbers of their bank accounts were observable, which was consistent with a standard security protocol to safeguard them. Once that was accomplished, it wasn't hard to make a match. "Yes," he said in triumph and turned toward Marcie, who appeared engrossed in her screen, and announced, "I think I found our culprit."

CHAPTER 35

One of the day guards escorted Frank and Dasha into the apartment building's audiovisual room. The space was long and narrow and two-tiered with the upper level being more of a viewing station. The walls were painted light gray. They were greeted by two other watchmen, who briefly turned away from their collection of monitors. "Have a seat," the guard closest to the door said, motioning to empty chairs in the area behind them. He added, "We have freshly brewed coffee."

Dasha waved her hand. "No, thank you, for now. Maybe later."

"My name is Jack," the nearby guard said forgoing a customary handshake. "My partner's name is Bud."

Bud waved.

"Pleased to meet you. I'm Dasha, and this is my colleague, Frank."

Jack nodded. "I've been briefed about your assignment, but not what's it all about, only that you are keeping tabs on an unnamed woman."

"Her name is unimportant. Our only interest is finding out who she is visiting in this building," Dasha said while eyeing the array of CCTV screens. "I see each of the locations is labeled. Right now, we want to see which entrance she uses and where she goes once inside the building."

"Do you have any idea when she will arrive?" Jack asked.

"Within the hour," Frank cut in.

"Do you know most of the tenants by sight?" Dasha asked.

"Ha," Bud said, "That's over five hundred people. Hard to remember them all. Except for the good looking ones. Right, Jack?"

Jack snorted. "It was easier when we could use our facial recognition program. But, you know, everyone here is supersensitive about privacy."

"Do you ever have problems?" Frank asked.

"Nope," Jack replied, then frowned. "Well, we do have an occasional drunk to deal with, but that's about it."

When clusters of people began arriving at various entrances, everyone in the room concentrated on the monitors. Slowly the residents or guests departed the lobbies and disappeared into one of the trio of elevators. The hectic flow continued for at least an hour as people entered and reappeared on other monitors that revealed them stepping onto their floors and eventually into their residences.

"There she is!" Dasha shouted and pointed. "Do either of you know who that guy is that's with her?"

"Yeah, I've seen him before," Bud said. "Don't know his name, but I don't think I've ever seen that woman before."

"Yep, I'd certainly remember that body," said Jack, as he braced himself in his chair.

"Let's keep a close eye on which floor they get off," Frank said, rising from his chair.

"Each corridor has a camera that is motion activated. As soon as they get off, we'll get a live picture of 'em," Bud replied.

Ignoring the comings and goings of the others, everyone in that room stayed focused. After several minutes waiting for the couple to walk out, Dasha said, "Where'd they go?"

Just as baffled, Frank asked, "Is it possible that one of your cameras may not be working or have any blind spots?"

Jack shook his head. "Absolutely not. Every inch of those floors is covered. If there's a malfunction of the equipment, an alarm will sound in this room."

"Well, they just couldn't have disappeared into thin air," Dasha moaned.

Frank scratched his head. "What goes up, must come down. Marcie Reynolds has to work. So, I'm guessing that we'll have to hang around here until she leaves."

"I guess you're right, but then what?" Dasha asked.

"I don't know," Frank said. "Maybe not seeing them leave the elevator was just a glitch in the system. We don't have a choice, we'll have to wait and see."

The next few hours were spent in idle chatter supplemented with coffee. Finding the confinement claustrophobic, Frank got up and decided to go for a walk. He did not share Dasha's enthusiasm for surveillance work and wished he was allowed to practice his skill as a literary agent instead of being a detective.

Outside the audiovisual room, occasionally, he would greet a tenant who would glance at him with apparent uneasiness. His salutation would, more often, be returned with some hesitancy. He thought, maybe it was his manner, his look of not belonging— something that he truly believed. That thought of not belonging gnawed at his psyche. Like a dog who doesn't know of any other option, but to return to its master, Frank joined Dasha in the audiovisual room.

"Anything happen, yet?" Frank asked.

"No, sir," Bud replied.

Dasha remained silent, but her look of annoyance told Frank she was losing patience.

"There!" Jack pointed to the ground floor's monitor. "There she is. Damn, how the hell did she do that?"

"She appeared just as mysteriously as she disappeared," Bud said, rising to his feet.

Everyone in the room followed suit and stood in surprise as Marcie Reynolds sashayed her way out of the building.

CHAPTER 36

Frank and Dasha stood mute as Samantha Brighton digested the written report she had just finished reading. Flipping it aside, she said, "I've had enough of this cat-and-mouse game. I want action."

"What do you suggest?" Dasha asked.

"Maybe we should throw a party for her and see if her mysterious friend shows up."

Dasha and Frank exchanged glances.

Brighton's face reddened. "I'm being sarcastic," she barked. "I want her, and you two are going to get her for me."

"By force?" Frank asked.

Brighton slammed the desk with her fist. "By any means. Got that? By *any means*."

Dasha moved uneasily in place. "Shouldn't the CAS agents handle that? After all, they are the only ones who are authorized to carry weapons."

Brighton rose from her chair and moved toward a side cabinet. Using a security card, she opened a drawer, swiped the card again, and accessed a safe. She reached in and pulled out a gun. Returning to her desk, she placed it on its surface. "Either of you ever fire any type of weapon?"

Frank had no memory of using such a weapon.

"I did," Dasha said, "while training for my position."

Brighton smiled. "Good. This is the M-17, and it's loaded with all the ammo that you'll need. It's a bit of an antique, but it works. If the intimidation factor isn't enough, it has enough power to drop an attacker. After you corner Marcie Reynolds, I want you to put these on her and bring her in." She pulled out a pair of electronic handcuffs from her center desk drawer and placed them alongside the weapon. Brighton tapped them with her index finger. "If Marcie Reynolds becomes unruly, these have built-in electric shock capabilities."

"Haven't those been outlawed?" asked Dasha.

"Let me worry about the legalities. You just do your job," Brighton said and handed the remote control to Dasha.

"What are the, uh, charges?" Frank asked, mentally bracing for blowback.

"That's a good point."

Her openness to his question surprised him.

"You're not going to arrest her. You're going to kidnap her."

Frank was stunned. He looked at Dasha, who appeared to take it in stride.

Dasha asked, "What do we do when we catch her?"

Brighton fumbled in her desk drawer and pulled out a small piece of paper. "As of this moment, I will not be communicating with you electronically. The address of the place is on this." She slid the note over to Dasha. "Memorize this. I don't want any trail coming back to me. Got that?"

Frank and Dasha nodded.

Dasha studied the note and handed it back. "What about the CAS agents?"

Brighton stuck the piece of paper into the nearby shredder. "I've called them off. The only reports they give me are pathetic. They note her movements, but they're too dense to connect the dots."

Frank began to feel more at ease. "What reason did you give them for canceling the surveillance?"

"You do ask some pretty good questions, Frank."

Frank smiled and glanced at Dasha, hoping to see her support, instead, he noticed her staring out the window.

"I told them that the missing data had been recovered, and Marcie Reynolds was no longer a suspect."

Dasha asked, "Didn't they want to know who it was or how it was retrieved?"

"They did. I told my CAS contact that an anonymous source told me where I could find the capsule. I also disclosed to her that the unidentified person was afraid of the consequences of stealing the data and just wanted to return it so we would stop looking for it."

"It's all well and good, but what if the stuff shows up and is made public? Won't that place you under scrutiny and make you a suspect?" Frank asked.

Brighton narrowed her gaze. "That's why I'm sending you two on this mission to make sure that doesn't happen. I'm counting on it. Understand?"

Frank cleared his throat. "I understand."

"Okay, now that we *understand* each other, I want this done tomorrow morning after Reynolds gets off her shift. I don't care where you do it, but avoid the CCTV cameras."

Dasha spoke up. "What's the purpose of capturing Reynolds? Are we going to make her talk by torturing her into giving up her accomplice?"

Samantha Brighton's eyes lit up. "No, we are going to use her as bait."

CHAPTER 37

Joe escorted Marcie into his apartment and gave her a welcoming kiss. Knowing they had a limited amount of time, Marcie moved quickly to her workstation. "I'm eager to get back to this Brahe Project." She flipped on her computer and waited as the screen glowed to life. "This stuff is fascinating."

"I hope that memory stick isn't going to get more attention than me," Joe said, feigning jealousy.

She repaid his suspicion with a smile. "You don't have to ever worry about that, lover boy."

Chuckling, Joe moved to pick up a sheet of paper. "While you were at work, I ran a trace on those bank account numbers."

"And?"

"At this point, I can't be sure. Some of the lottery funds are going into bank accounts other than those of the winners—that's for certain. *And* that person may be working for the Central Consortium. Of course, I only have the last four digits to cross-reference. Because of the repetition by a couple of people, I won't know until I actually tap into those individual accounts."

"How do you intend to do that?"

Joe settled back in his chair. "Every system has a weak link. In this case, it's the cafeteria's credit card system, that I'll use to penetrate the bank's defenses. Once inside, I'll leapfrog into various accounts until I find a match."

"That sounds like work. Isn't that going to take a lot of time, I mean, the number of bank account numbers ..."

"I don't do all the work. The computer does most of it. After I'm in, my program will automatically reprocess my probe thousands of times."

"But how do you hack your way in? Since companies use pneumatic data transfer, you can't extract information like the old days of the internet."

"All the people in this building have connections, and that includes banks. Most of them have personal links to their financial institutions. That direct-line matrix gives them a sense of security. Under normal circumstances, it would guarantee them privacy, but I have succeeded in commandeering that system for my own use. Having access to all the major monetary institutions gives me the freedom to search multiple databases, all from the comfort of this chair."

Marcie looked stunned and regarded Joe with an unfocused gaze. "That's incredible."

"I've been waiting years for this moment. This is my revenge for my brother's death."

Joe turned toward his computer. Marcie followed his lead and returned to her project.

Engrossed in their work, few words passed between them for some time until Joe glanced up and took note of a rapidly flashing red light above his console. "Someone's heading to this floor on the elevator."

"Is that a problem?" Marcie asked.

"I don't think so. It's just unusual for this time of day." Joe switched on an overhead monitor. "This is strange." He became alarmed as he saw four guards exit the elevator. He rose to his feet and cranked his head upward toward the screen. He sat again. "They appear to be looking for something." He ran his fingers through his hair.

"Us?"

"Maybe ... I don't know." He jumped up again. "They shouldn't be able to hear us behind my entrance barrier." Joe eyed Marcie and gave her a forced smile. He knew he was cornered. His pulse quicked. He inhaled deeply and started to pace in front of the monitor. Occasionally, he would glance at his watch.

Marcie nervously scanned the interior. "I suppose there's only one way in and one way out of this place?"

"Yep, if you don't consider the roof hatch." Joe was unnerved by the situation. He switched on two other monitors. As the guards spread out and continued to explore, every screen was filled with activity. Each man held a flashlight; their probing beams flayed at the mechanical room's floor and walls. One of the cameras snared a shaft of light, momentarily disabling it. Joe's pulse raced, and with bated breath, he watched.

The screen slowly returned to normal.

They kept their eyes trained on the CCTV monitors.

Marcie slowly moved toward Joe. "What do we do if they get in?"

"They won't."

Marcie looked at her watch. "I can't stay here forever. At some point, I have to leave."

"We can't panic. Let's see what happens." Inside, Joe felt just the opposite of his feigned reassurance.

"I'd like to say no matter, but do you have a plan if they break in?"

Joe moved toward his desk and pulled out a revolver. "Those guards are not armed. This is my only option."

"A gun!" she gasped and recoiled. "It's a capital offense to even own one."

"You asked me if I had a plan—this is it," he said before tucking it back into the drawer.

"Let's hope it doesn't come to that."

Joe turned away from Marcie and noticed the guards regrouping near the elevator. One of the men pushed the call button, while another spoke into his shoulder microphone. As they waited for the elevator to arrive the men appeared to maintain interest in their surroundings.

Joe looked at Marcie. "You can't leave now. I think it's best that you stay here for a while."

"When do you think it'll be safe?"

"There's a lot of activity when many of the residents return from work. I think that'll be a good time for you to blend into the crowd."

Marcie shrugged. "No matter, but right now, I could use something stronger than a Molson."

"Scotch?"

"Double."

Joe gave Marcie a sympathetic smile. "Yeah, me too. Let's go into the sitting room. We can come back here after we wind down."

After Joe served their drinks, he took his place next to her. She took a quick sip and instinctively cuddled up to him. "I've had more excitement in the past couple of weeks than in my entire lifetime."

"Yeah, and that's what's bothering me."

"What do you mean, Joe?"

"This is the first time a group of security goons came to my floor nosing around. There has to be a reason."

"You don't think I had anything to do with it?"

Joe shook his head. "No, not at all, but you may be the reason. Where's that phone I gave you?"

"In my purse."

"Can you get it for me?"

"Now?"

"Yeah, most definitely now."

Marcie returned and handed the phone to Joe and resumed sitting next to him.

Joe slid open a side part of the phone and removed its SIM card. He snapped it in two and discarded it on a side table. He then removed its battery and placed it alongside the rest of the phone. Joe handed her a new phone. "I think I've solved the problem."

CHAPTER 38

Frank pointed beyond the car's windshield. "There she is."

Dasha nodded. "I see that, but our proximity alarm didn't alert us. Something's wrong."

"Like what?"

Playing with her tracker, Dasha said, "Either she left it behind, or it's no longer functioning. In either case, we don't have the advantage of keeping a close watch on Marcie Reynolds."

"We're still able to track her car."

"As long as she's in it, Frank."

They watched as Reynolds crossed the street and got into her car. Once she was underway, Dasha followed at a safe distance.

Frank eyed his watch. "I'm guessing, by this time of night, she's heading for work."

"No doubt about it, Frank. According to Brighton's orders, we have to get her soon."

"I'm tired of being stuck in a cramped car."

"Me, too. Either we get Reynolds now, before her shift, or wait around for another nine hours."

"You're the one with the gun. I'd say now would be as good of a time as any."

Dasha began to accelerate. "Frank, brace yourself for the ride of your life." For a moment, their vehicle came alongside Reynolds' car but only matched her speed for a few seconds before zooming past.

"You're not going to follow her?"

"No. I have a better plan."

Frank saw the resolve in Dasha behavior. She leaned forward, her eyes darting between the road in front and her rearview camera's screen. Soon she outpaced Reynolds and took a sharp turn onto a side street.

Glancing back, Frank asked, "Where are you going?"

"She's a creature of habit. I have a plan. Get that M17 out of my purse and put it on the dash."

He carefully removed the gun and placed it in the depression below the windshield.

Keeping one hand on the steering wheel, she flipped on the autopilot. With both hands free, Dasha grabbed the weapon and rammed in the first round. She made sure the safety was still on and placed the pistol on her lap.

"You seem to handle that quite well," Frank said as he nervously continued to consider their situation.

"Top in my class."

Frank pointed to the handgun. "You plan on using that?"

She laughed. "What, and have Brighton pissed? No, it's merely a mind-changer. Remember, she's no use to us dead."

Dasha turned off the autopilot. "Hang on. Here we go."

Frank felt the car surge forward. It banked to the left, traveled down an alleyway and abruptly came to a stop before an intersection. Dasha killed the lights, but continued to rev the engine.

"Here she comes," Dasha said.

Marcie Reynolds' auto-assisted breaks screeched to a halt as Dasha turned her car into the intersection. With high beams blazing, Marcie instinctively raised her arms to deflect the glare.

Dasha grabbed the gun, sprung out of the vehicle, and yelled. "Now, Frank!" She ran to the driver's side and pointed the M17 at Reynolds' head. "Get out!"

Reynolds, clearly stunned, squinted at Dasha. "What?"

"I said, get out! Now!"

Frank, himself confused by the unexpectedness of Dasha's maneuver, moved to the passenger side but was unable to open the door.

Frozen, either by fear or confusion, Marcie continued to hold her position.

Dasha fired a single round through the rear passenger side window. Shards of glass, like tiny jagged diamonds, littered the back seat.

Marcie flinched. She unlocked the door and began to step out of the car.

Frank, his ears throbbing from the gunshot, pulled out the pair of handcuffs from his pocket. He ran over to Dasha, who kept her gun trained on Marcie Reynolds.

"Cuff her, Frank," Dasha ordered. "We've got to get the hell out of here."

With Marcie's hands manacled behind her back, Dasha blindfolded her, then roughly guided her to Dasha's vehicle. "Frank, take her car and follow us."

In the distance, the sound of approaching sirens spurred them on, as they hastily disappeared into the shadowy criminal netherworld of Old Town.

Frank kept his eyes trained on Dasha's car as she maneuvered it through the back alleys of the town. His clammy hands firmly gripped the steering wheel. Occasionally, he could see the silhouettes of Dash's and Marcie's heads as they bobbing back and forth, backlit by a chance encounter with an approaching vehicle.

He heard the whistle of air from Dasha's single shot. Although small, the spidering fractures of glass from its center were bound to draw attention. He reached over and pushed a button to lower the window to hide it from view. It was a chilly evening, and the current of cold air that moved within the interior did little to lessen the moisture on Frank's clammy hands.

Dasha moved her car down a narrow lane and stopped in front of a two-car garage. The door rose, she guided her vehicle into one of the parking spots. Dasha was already outside her automobile by the time Frank came to a stop alongside her car.

As the garage door began to close, Frank helped Marcie Reynolds out of her seat while Dasha trained her M17 on her. Only the faint glow from a nearby nightlight illuminated them. Dasha yanked off Marcie Reynolds' head covering and threw it back onto the car's seat.

"I remember you two," Marcie said, trying to twist away from Frank's grip.

"Easy, now, Ms. Reynolds," Dasha said, pointing her gun directly at Reynolds' face.

"You aren't the police. What do you want from me?"

Dasha coaxed Reynolds along with a sweeping motion from her weapon. "Get moving. You'll find out soon enough."

The three of them moved toward the back of the garage, with Frank holding point. Dasha gripped Marcie's manacled hands while keeping her gun trained on her spine. Frank, in the lead, opened the rear door, letting Dasha and Marcie pass before following them down a narrow hallway that emptied into a dining room.

Frank fumbled for the light switch. Locating it, a shoddy looking chandelier, with four of its six lights inoperative, dimly lit the interior.

Dasha grabbed a chair, turned it around to face Marcie. "Sit!" she ordered.

Marcie mocked. "You know, even having a gun is a crime … punishable by death."

"Shut up," Dasha barked. "You're not here to discuss the law." She placed the M-17 on a nearby countertop. From her purse, she pulled out the handcuffs' remote control and callously pushed a button.

Marcie shrieked.

Dasha moved closer to Marcie and intimidated her by waving the device in her face. "I want some answers."

With frightened eyes, Marcie asked, "Okay, why am I here?"

"Frank, get her purse from the car."

He nodded and hurriedly left. Returning, he placed it in the center of the dining room table.

Dasha moved behind Marcie and rested the remote on the table. Taking the handbag by the bottom, she unceremoniously flipped it over, letting its contents spill onto the table. Dasha shook it several times before reaching in to pull out the remains that were too tightly wedged inside. Next, she unfastened all pockets and dumped odds and ends on top of the growing pile.

Among the collection of feminine paraphernalia were two cell phones. Dasha took particular attention to the dated model. She flipped it open and studied its screen. Returning to face Marcie Reynolds, Dasha shook it at her. "What's this?" she yelled.

Marcie laughed. "It's a mobile phone."

No longer holding the controller, she gave Marcie a backhand slap across the face, drawing a trickle of blood. "This is no joke. Why do you have this invalid phone, and who do you call with it?"

Frank was stunned by Dasha's aggressiveness.

"It's just an old phone."

Dasha raised her foot and struck Marcie in the midriff.

Marcie wheezed.

While Marcie continued to labor for air, Dasha flipped open the phone again. She found only one entry in its directory. Facing the screen toward Marcie, she asked forcefully, "Who's 'Me?'"

Marcie Reynolds' cold eyes glared at her with contempt. Spitting at Dasha, she said, "Go to hell!" Spittle and blood dripped from her lips.

Dasha raised her foot again and thrust it at Reynolds' chest. Marcie's chair teetered backward. Dasha gave her one more shove. Marcie's head grazed the edge of the dining room table before she fell sideways onto the carpeted floor.

CHAPTER 39

Joe awakened to the sound of his phone. Bleary-eyed, the glow from the screen made him squint. "Hi, it's only been a couple of hours," he said as he propped himself up against the backboard. "Miss me already?"

"Hey, sweetie," an unfamiliar female's voice greeted.

"Who is this?" he asked forcefully.

"This is your worst nightmare, and its gonna get rougher if you don't cooperate."

There was a protracted pause, his gut feeling told him to attack, but he forced himself to remain calm. *Don't take the bait.* Joe asked calmly but forcefully, "What do you want? Where is Marcie?"

"Listen, sweetie, I'll get to the point. We're holding Marcie Reynolds in exchange for all those memory sticks you stole. You have exactly twenty-four hours to turn everything over—copies and notes. If you don't, your girlfriend is going to have some reconstructive surgery done to that beautiful face of hers."

Joe's heart raced. He flung his covers aside and swung out of bed. He released his pent-up anger. "Listen, you bitch, you're not holding the cards you think you're holding." He punched the end call icon and threw his phone onto the bed. Having second thoughts, he retrieved the phone and removed the SIM card and battery.

Now, fully awake and fuming, he dashed to his workstation and fired up his computer. Waiting for the screen to brighten, he gathered his notes and mentally readied himself for what he expected was going to be a long night.

Joe resumed his cross-reference data with bank account numbers, matching them with the cafeteria records. Knowing Marcie's life depended on what he was doing, he checked and verified the result. After hours of staring at his computer's screen, Joe triumphantly sat back in his chair and breathed a sigh of relief. "I'll show you who's going to have a new facial," he muttered to himself.

Joe checked the time. In less than a couple of hours, the building was about to buzz with activity as people went to work. He gathered his printouts and shoved them into a briefcase, retrieved his revolver, and placed it alongside the case. In need of rejuvenation, he headed for the shower.

***

With his phone reactivated, Joe sat in a hotel parking lot, his car camouflaged among other nondescript vehicles. He hit redial. The response on the other end was immediate.

"Hi, sweetie. So, you've come to your senses."

Joe bristled at being called *sweetie.* "Yeah," Joe answered tersely. "I want to talk to Marcie. Put her on."

Following a moment of silence, Marcie said with some hesitation, "Hi … I'm all right … just tired."

"Don't worry, I'll handle everything—"

"I'm back, sweetie. So, you have everything we asked for?"

"Yeah … then some."

"Okay, sweetie, we meet in Henderson Park's main pavilion to make the exchange."

"How soon?"

"One   hour?"

"Okay, but I pick the spot."

"We're calling the shots, sweetie—one hour—Henderson Park."

Joe clenched his jaw. "One hour—Long View Scenic Overlook on Lakeshore Road. And I don't care where you're going … I just told you where I'll be." He ended the conversation with a click. Again, he removed the phone's SIM card and battery.

***

Joe arrived at the rendezvous site and selected a parking space near the exit, far away from the viewing rail. He wanted a spot that gave him an advantage for an easy escape if he needed one. Having reached his destination well in advance of the meeting, he scrutinized each visitor that came and went, unsure what accomplices would be involved in the operation.

He rolled down both front windows. Despite the bright sunshine, a cool breeze flowed across the car's interior. He partially zipped up his jacket, then reached inside the right side pocket for the reassuring contact with his revolver. He glanced at his watch. *Five more minutes.*

Even though Joe had carefully laid his briefcase on the front seat, his nervousness prompted him to slightly reposition it. It was more of an activity to occupy his time than dissatisfaction with its original placement. He looked at his watch again. *Two more minutes.*

A vehicle with three passengers turned off the highway and into the lot, leaving behind a short tail of sand in its wake. As it circled, the car's windshield caught the bright rays of the sun, partially obscuring the identity of those inside. Not until the vehicle came to rest did he recognize Marcie as one of its occupants.

The driver chose a spot two car widths away. Joe remained seated, expecting someone from the car to make the first move. The car parked parallel to Joe's with the driver's side facing him. Joe was thankful that it still left his vehicle open for a quick retreat. The driver stepped out and moved halfway toward him. Joe figured the woman to be the chief negotiator. She was tall and shapely, With her auburn hair tied in a bun, she possessed the cunningness of a fox as she approached. He opened his door but remained behind it. Joe rested his arms on the top frame of the door.

Joe asked, "What's your name?"

"Hi, sweetie. Let's be informal. You can call me Dasha."

Joe felt a heaviness in his stomach at her mocking. He chose his alias. "Gary Duprey."

Dasha smirked. "C'mon now, I know that's false, but I'll let that go. You have the stuff?"

"Yeah, right here on the front seat." Joe obliquely pointed behind him, then slid his hand into his jacket pocket for his gun. He looked over the parking lot again and saw only one other vehicle perched near the edge of the overlook's guardrail. "Before I give you anything, I want Marcie to come out so I can see that she's all right."

Dasha signaled toward her car. The door opened, and Marcie stepped out with none other than Rodney Bells close behind. Like their brief encounter at the elevator, he showed no sign of recognizing Joe. Marcie looked haggard.

"Okay, *Mr. Duprey,* now it's your turn."

Joe turned and picked up the briefcase from the front seat. He then left the protective cover of the car door and laid the case on the car's hood. Joe leaned back against the vehicle's front end. "Your move," he said.

Dasha moved near Rodney and whispered something into his ear. Leaving Marcie with Dasha, Rodney began to approach Joe. Within a few feet of him, Rodney said, "Hand the briefcase over."

"Okay, Rodney," Joe said, paying close attention to his reaction. Joe observed a flicker of recall in his eyes.

"My name's Frank, mister."

"Whatever you say, *Frank*." Joe turned for the case, pulled it across the hood, and held it out to him.

Frank, a.k.a. Rodney Bells, took it and began to back away. Stopping alongside Dasha, he traded places with her and grabbed Marcie by the arm.

Dasha promptly opened it and looked inside. Her eyes, now riveted on Joe, were seething. "Is this some sort of a joke?" she yelled.

"I guess it is, Charlotte Piper. And I suppose it's on the CanAmerican government, too."

Dasha's superior smirk abruptly warped into a snarl. Her eyes narrowed into piggy slits. "My name is Dasha Kozar!"

"Yell all you want, Charlotte. The con's up. Unless …" Joe intentionally allowed his tacit proposal to linger, expecting her to nibble at the bait.

Baring her teeth like a cornered animal, she snapped, "Unless what?"

"Unless you release Marcie, I will reveal how you and Charlotte are one and the same."

Dasha reached inside her coat pocket and partially flashed the M-17 in his direction before slipping it back.

"I don't think you're that stupid," Joe revealed his gun. "A gun battle is going to draw a

lot of attention, and there's only one way out of here. Besides, even if you kill Marcie and me, I've arranged for an info dump on The Wall. That will certainly draw more attention to you than gunfire."

Dasha's intimidating stare dissolved. "Who's to say you're not going to do that anyway?"

"I could say 'you have my word,' you know, honor among thieves." Joe gave her a sardonic grin.

To Joe, Frank appeared more like a movie extra who needed coaxing. Joe saw Frank's bewildered gaze skip from him to Dasha.

Dasha's confrontational attitude relaxed. "Frank, let her go."

Frank shot Dasha a puzzled look.

"I said, let her go."

Frank released his grip, and Marcie promptly moved toward Joe. She hurriedly went to the passenger's side of the car and got in.

"Charlotte ... Dasha, or whatever you like to call yourself, Marcie is going on a two-week vacation. Make sure you arrange the paperwork. When she returns, everything is going to be back to normal.   Got   that?"

Dasha started to back away and move toward her vehicle. "You may think you're holding the cards now, sweetie, but if you cross me, both you and your honey will regret it."

Joe laughed. "What we have here is a stalemate."

"We'll see who blinks first, sweetie."

CHAPTER 40

Frank studied Dasha as she maneuvered back onto the highway. Her cockiness gone, she stared at the oncoming traffic with cold, calculating eyes. Frank saw her hands tighten on the steering wheel as she rocketed past slower vehicles.

Sensing her irritation, he cautiously asked, "What's next?"

His question fell on deaf ears. Dasha pushed harder on the accelerator. Frank stiffened in his seat.

Uncomfortable with the silence and vehicle's zigzagging, he probed again, hoping to alleviate her fury. "Why did that guy call me Rodney?"

Dasha attention remained riveted on the freeway's flow. Governed by the increase in traffic she eased up on the controller and put in into self-driving mode. She pursed her lips. "I don't know," she said defensively. "Maybe he thought you were someone else."

"He appeared pretty sure of himself."

Dasha barked, "We have more to worry about than mistaken identity. Brighton is going to be pissed when we tell her what happened."

Frank turned and looked directly at Dasha, but she did not look at him. "Yeah, what did happen?" he asked forcefully.

Still focused ahead, she said, "A shakedown."

"So it's true, what he said, that you and Charlotte Piper are one and the same?"

"I'd suggest you mind your own business. Brighton and I will handle this matter."

Dasha's harsh chiding did not sit well with Frank. The unbroken silence that followed served to foster Frank's suspicion about her real objectives concerning him. No longer hostile, but troubled by recent events, he began to consider his options.

***

Samantha Brighton remained motionless as Dasha Kozar finished telling her what happened.

Appearing to contain her emotion throughout the narrative, Brighton's outburst became explosive. "Damn it! Damn it! Damn it! If this leaks out, we're done for. Nothing has been going right for us." She slapped her hand on the desk.

Dasha cleared her throat. "There is one bright outcome in all of this."

Brighton looked at her with puzzlement. "What could possibly be beneficial in this whole mess?"

"Frank identified his partner in the guerrilla network. This guy, Gary Duprey, recognized Frank and called him Rodney."

Brighton's jaw dropped. "What was Frank's reaction?"

"I don't think he reacted, other than asking me why Duprey called him by that name."

Pushing herself away from her desk, Brighton rose and moved toward her office window. Staring out at the sea of buildings, she said, "Okay, let's think this through. Right now, Gary Duprey is blackmailing us. If we leave him alone and his turncoat Marcie Reynolds, our secret is safe."

"I don't like living under a cloud, constantly looking over my shoulder."

Brighton turned her attention to Dasha. "Nor do I. When you think about it, having them call the shots puts us in an unimaginable position."

"Now that we know one of the ringleaders in the rebel group, why can't we notify CAS and have them arrested for treason?"

Brighton returned to her desk but remained standing. "And then what, have them spill their guts to the authorities, and we end up being guillotined in Quebec, along with them?" Her voice began to rise. "I'm not going to lose my head over those bastards."

Dasha sighed and rose from her chair. "Then what do we do?"

Brighton opened the top drawer of her desk and removed something. She began to slowly walk toward Dasha. "We eliminate the problem," she said with grim firmness and handed Dasha a silencer for the M-17.

"By that, you mean … "

"Exactly," Brighton said before giving Dasha a parting kiss.

CHAPTER 41

Joe held the door open for Marcie as she entered Joe's Old Town hideaway. She went over to the couch, propped a pillow at one end, and collapsed. She grimaced.

"What's wrong?" Joe asked.

"No matter. I didn't want to worry you and say anything earlier. Things got a little physical."

"What do you mean, 'physical?'"

Marcie lifted her blouse. Exposing her midriff, Joe saw it was covered with numerous black and blue marks. "Did that bastard, Frank, do that?"

Her usual exuberant demeanor gone, she shook her head slowly. "No, it was that woman, Dasha. She's a psycho."

"What about that guy, the one called Frank?"

"Not really much to say about him. He just followed orders. Dasha did all the beating. Why did you call him Rodney?"

"Let me get you some ice first."

Pointing to the back of her head, she said, "I could use some here, too."

Joe went to the linen cabinet and retrieved a couple of towels before going to the freezer. He grabbed some ice and wrapped them, making a proper icepack. Joe carefully rested it on Marcie's exposed belly. "There, that should help," he said, looking at her with concern. "Now for your head." He handed her the other bundle.

Marcie applied it to her head and smiled. "Thanks. You're a good nurse."

Joe smiled back and sat down beside Marcie, resting his hand on hers. "Now that I've taken care of that, I'll tell you about Rodney Bells. I've known him for many years. We were active in the resistance. Rodney acted as our publicity man. Once we discovered something criminal going on, within the régime, we publicized it on all social media, and when we could, governmental sources. It became a game of catch me if you can." Joe laughed.

"Why didn't Rodney recognize you?"

"I'm not sure. About three years ago, we discovered irregularities within certain governmental agencies, but we couldn't pinpoint who was doing what. Since the development of the pneumatic records transfer, we could no longer tap directly into those secure networks and recover classified data."

"But, what about your access to all the government administrators' personal accounts within your building?"

"That only works to a certain point. The bridge between important data is via the tube network. And that was almost impossible to crack. That was until the development of the pressure stabilizing tap, which I invented."

Marcie nodded approvingly. "As an engineer, I do admire your creativity. But you're still not telling me about Rodney Bells. What's his story?"

"Okay, we were going to use my invention about a year ago. Somehow, I think maybe because of an informant, our plan to intercept a data capsule was discovered. Rodney was doing some reconnaissance for the mission, and I assumed he was captured."

"Assumed?"

"Yeah. When Rodney never reported back, I assumed that's what happened. He just dropped off the radar. It wasn't until I spotted Rodney working at Central Consortium's headquarters that I saw he was alive and well. And at that point, I was unsure whose side he was on."

Marcie removed both ice packs and handed them to Joe. "It's a bit too cold. I think that's enough for now. How many people are in the resistance?"

Joe dropped the wet towels into the sink and returned to Marcie's side before he spoke. "Hundreds, maybe thousands. No one knows exactly the real number."

Marcie's eyes widened. "How do you correspond with one another?"

"That's the beautiful thing. There's no central command. But we do have a commonality of purpose. Maybe two or three of us form a cell, but all communication is strictly by word of mouth or paper. And the written text is destroyed immediately after it is delivered."

"What's their motivation?"

"Everyone of us has been harmed by the CanAmerican Union. We each have some reason to see it destroyed. Little by little, we are undermining the system."

"And your reason?" Marcie asked.

"I already told you. My brother's death motivates me, and that's all I'll say for now."

Marcie pushed herself into a sitting position and gave Joe a kiss. "No matter. I'll be here if you ever want to talk about it."

Joe rose. "Care for something to eat?"

"Yes! I'm famished, but I think the soup would be a good start for now."

From across the room, he said, "Since you came here last, I've added more provisions. I hope you like chicken noodle soup?"

"My favorite. And speaking of food, I assume we can't stay here forever. What's our next move?"

Joe rummaged for a pan. "I have to temporarily relocate our operation here for the time being."

"What about your computers and records?"

"I've been thinking about that. Right now we are in a mutual destruction standoff with that woman, Dasha, and someone else in Central Consortium. That won't last forever. We need to take advantage of the lull and gather what we can from my apartment."

Marcie eased herself off the couch and moved toward Joe. She rested an arm on his shoulder. "No matter. For me, there's no turning back." She kissed him on the cheek.

He set the pot aside and embraced her. "I've been living on the edge for several years, now. I couldn't turn back if I wanted to." Joe kissed her on the lips and drew back, admiring her face. "Now that I have you, my outlook on life has changed."

"Mine, too," Marcie said before she drew him back to her.

CHAPTER 42

When Dasha entered Frank's office, he remained seated. Instead of acknowledging her, Frank focused on the sun's departure and the lengthening shadows of the imposing buildings. He deliberated on the increasing number of points of light that melted into the cold, dark veneer of the structures—likely the tells of persons free from their labors. *Where are they going? Family? Friends?*

Dasha cleared her throat. "Um … Frank?"

Frank pivoted his chair toward her. "I've been thinking about what happened today."

"And?"

"And I don't like it."

She threw her arms into the air. "I don't like it either, but it's what we are ordered to do. You understand these people are terrorists, don't you?"

"You certainly didn't have to kick that woman."

Frowning, Dasha crossed her arms over her chest and moved toward the window. Not looking directly at him, but outside at the remnants of daylight, she said, "I had to try and make her talk."

"Why didn't you use the handcuff's zapper?"

"I didn't have it in my hand at the time. It was an emotional response," Dasha snapped.

"And she didn't talk, did she?"

Whirling around, Dasha thrust out a menacing index finger in Frank's face and fumed.

"That's not the point!"

Frank recoiled as if confronted by a snake.

Appearing startled by his reaction, she withdrew to sit in one of the loungers on the other side of the room. She crossed her legs and drummed her fingers on its armrest. Her mood appeared to soften. "I'm sorry, Frank. I didn't mean to lose my temper." She pointed to the other matching chair. "Come, sit over there."

Reluctantly, he took a seat.

Dasha gathered her hands on her lap and shifted uneasily in place. "Frank," she began in an almost beseeching manner. "I need your help. I find this whole business troubling. The Can-American Union is fighting for its very existence. These people that we are dealing with are evil and need to be stopped."

"Why not involve CAS?" he asked, meeting her gaze with skepticism.

She looked up at him. "Because Samantha Brighton believes they may be part of the coup."

"If that's the case, what's the solution?"

"There's only one solution, and I think you know what that is," Dasha said coldly.

CHAPTER 43

Using a stolen van, Joe and Marcie backed into the loading pier of Joe's apartment building. Disguised as an HVAC team, they presented their falsified credentials to the dock security guard.

"I wasn't aware we had a problem," the guard said, glancing at the bogus work order.

"Listen," Joe said smartly, "all I know is that we received an emergency alert that the centrifugal fan is going to fail soon if we don't repair your central plant's system."

"I ... I don't know. We usually get a notice you guys are coming."

"Okay ... " Joe looked at the man's name tag. "Bill ... we'll go back and tell our boss that you won't let us check out the unit. When the part fails, which it soon will, you can explain that to your residents. I'm sure they won't be too happy with you." Joe turned and began to walk back to the front of the truck.

"Wait, a minute," the guard called out.

Joe turned back and regarded the watchman with impatience.

The burly guard gestured toward the service elevator in defeat and stepped aside.

"Thanks, Bill," Joe said as he opened the rear door to the van. "Nothing like keeping everyone happy. Right?"

The security guard nodded. "That's pretty big," he said, eyeing the cabinet.

"Has to be, with all the equipment, spare parts, and testing stuff," Joe said matter-of-factly.

With their cap visors pulled low to disguise their identity from the security cameras, Joe and Marcie rolled the toolbox onto the dock. Once in position, the guard pushed the call button. When the elevator arrived, it was apparent that it was going to be a tight fit for the two of them and the service cabinet. "We'll send it back down if you want to see what we're doing, but I don't usually advise that," Joe said, pushing while Marcie guided the cabinet inside. "There's always the risk of electrocution." He topped off the statement with a wink.

Joe received a wry smile from the guard as the elevator's doors scissored shut.

Feeling the upward lift, Joe watched Marcie study the ascending numbers. "Nervous?" he asked.

"A little, but I'm mostly tired."

"I'm sorry about that," he said sympathetically "I don't think we could have waited another day. By tomorrow they'll be in recovery mode and will be out for blood."

"Why not today?"

"Tonight they're licking their wounds and probably figuring out what to do next." The elevator bounced to a stop. The door yawned open. Joe stepped out and said, "At best, we only have a half-hour to gather computers, memory sticks, and hard drives. If we spend more time than that, I'm certain the watchman will get curious."

Marcie helped push the cabinet out. "No matter, I am just as eager to get out of here as you."

Joe said, "I'll grab all of the computers, and you take only two of the monitors." He pointed to the cabinet. "We should be able to fit everything in here."

Following the crooked corridor within the boundaries of ductwork, wire conduit, and steel girders, they pushed their empty Trojan horse to the other side of the mechanical room's floor. They passed the central elevator and continued on to the false wall of Joe's retreat.

The partition opened, and Joe and Marcie immediately entered, going directly to the computer room. Joe pointed and said, "Grab those monitors. I'll get the computers."

With the precision of a military operation, they completed their mission. After cramming all the workstation paraphernalia into the vacant space of the cabinet, they began to make their way back to the freight elevator. As they passed through the central part of the complex, Joe turned his head hurriedly, surprised at the arrival of the elevator.

"Done so soon?" Bill asked, eyeing them and the cart with a suggestion of mistrust in his behavior. He moved onto the floor and stood blocking Joe's way.

"You never really know about these calls. Yeah, it was only the controller board that needed to be swapped out," Joe said, wanting to continue to the other side of the floor.

The guard nodded sympathetically. "Yep, I understand. Before becoming a security guard," he pointed to his badge, "I used to be in the heating and cooling business, too. Couldn't take the climbing and crawling around anymore."

"Yeah," Joe said, "it's hard on the joints." Thinking the exchange over, he began to push the cabinet but was restrained by the heft of the man, who rested his arms on the leading end of it. The guard showed little sign of moving. Marcie, appearing hesitant, stood behind him, her arms akimbo, and waited.

The man, now fully maintaining his blockade, smacked his lips in reflection. "Ya know, pal, when I did this stuff, I had to go on the roof to switch out a defective controller board. And another thing, I didn't have to lug around such a big toolbox, either."

"Well, Bill," Joe said, "I'm sure things have changed since then." He then took an assertive stance and started to lean on his end of the cabinet.

"I'm kinda curious, what does the new controller look like?" asked the guard.

"No different than the old one, only placed inside and away from the elements."

"Hmm," the guard replied in obvious consideration. "I'd still like to have a look, Mister. And, you can consider this more of a demand than a request." The beefy man rose from his leaning position and moved to the side of the cabinet. He bent over and pulled open the side door.

Marcie, already primed for an altercation, grabbed a nearby fire extinguisher. Joe saw what she was about to do, and the shift in Joe's eyes must have alerted the guard. The man turned toward Marcie at the same time that she delivered a blow to his head. He hit the floor with a thump. "I figured that conversation had run its course," she said with a grin.

"That's one way of doing it. Now, before he comes to, let's use his belt to tie him up. It should buy us some time. He's pretty heavy, gimme a hand."

Joe and Marcie propped the man against a vertical strut. Utilizing the guard's belt and electrical wire from their toolbox, they secured him in place. After, they continued on their way when Joe stopped and ran back to the guard. He picked up the man's radio and returned to Marcie. He waved it at her. "This could come in handy."

On the ground floor, they moved their treasure-laden toolbox to the edge of the loading dock.

"Where's Bill?" a voice called out.

Joe turned and spotted another watchman approaching.

"He's coming. There's barely enough room for us and our toolbox. He said he had to see a man about a horse, or something like that."

The guard laughed. "That's Bill, always joking. Need a hand with that pal?"

Joe smiled. "Sure, why not. The more hands, the lighter the load."

After securing the cabinet, Marcie went forward into the front cab of the truck. Joe gave the guard a quick wave and joined her.

There was something in the way the guard looked at Joe, that made him uneasy, but Joe was long gone before it mattered.

CHAPTER 44

Dasha clicked off her earbud phone and removed it. Frank finished preparing a couple of drinks and looked at her with interest. "What was that all about?" he asked while drawing close to her and offering her one of the glasses.

She accepted the drink with poise, something Frank had not witnessed in her over the last couple of days. "Thank you," she said quietly. She sat on the far end of Frank's couch and curled her legs under her. "That was Samantha."

Frank was surprised by her usage of Brighton's first name. "By your reaction, I'd guess it wasn't good news." He chose a place on the opposite end of the couch. He noted her avoidance of eye contact with him.

"It wasn't," she murmured.

"Reynolds, and that guy?"

"Yes." She took a sip of scotch. "They went back to the apartment building. Why and for what is unclear, and they managed to knock out a watchman in the process. He ended up with a severe concussion."

"There has to be something very significant about that place for them to risk returning to that apartment building," said Frank.

"Samantha wants us to go back and find out what it is." Dasha drew her glass to her lips and swallowed hard. She winced.

"By the way you put away your scotch, I'd guess that's where we are headed right now."

"Yeah. Drink up Frank, it's time we put an end to this charade."

***

"I heard one of your guards got knocked out by one of them," Dasha said to Jack, the security chief, as she and Frank were escorted into the audiovisual room.

"Yep. Bill told me that he got suspicious when the HVAC techs didn't understand where the controller board was located. Actually, he said he was a bit apprehensive about them from the getgo."

Frank moved to a chair at the rear of the room.

"Bud, put on that footage from last night," Jack ordered.

129

One of the center monitors flickered, and the loading dock came into view. "Now keep an eye on them." Jack gestured toward the screen. "See how they try to keep those cap brims low over their faces. It's the same people we saw the other day."

"Didn't you recognize them from before?" Dasha asked.

"Hey, we don't live in this room twenty-four hours a day, lady. Our night shift was in this room."

"My name is Dasha Kozar, not *Lady*," she fired back.

"Sorry … Ms. Kozar. I guess my nerves are a little rattled." Jack, appearing mortified, turned toward the screen. "Bud, fast forward to when those two leave. Notice how they're straining to push that toolbox."

"Yeah," Frank said, "It's definitely heavier."

Dasha rose. "Take us to the top floor where your guard was attacked."

Bud remained seated while Jack led Frank and Dasha outside. "Follow me," Jack said. "The central elevator is closer, and it's actually where the confrontation occurred."

A tense silence accompanied them as they rode the car to the mechanical room. Jack was the first to step out. "This way," he said and directed Frank and Dasha around the corner. He pointed toward the fire extinguisher that lay on its side. "That's what they used to stop Bill."

Dasha gave it a quick glance.

Frank followed her movements and noticed wheel marks disappearing behind a wall. "Look at those tracks," he said. "It's pretty apparent to me that carts just don't go through walls. I'd say, whatever they came for is behind that." He pointed to the tan partition that was situated at the end of a series of holding tanks.

"You're right, Frank. What's on the other side of that?" Dasha asked, pointing toward the barrier.

Jack shrugged. "Don't know. I always thought it was just a wall. I have no idea what's on the other side. Maybe only ductwork."

Frank went over to it and gave the wall a forceful hit with the heel of his fist. "It's hollow!" he exclaimed.

"Most walls are," Jack said sarcastically.

Dasha yelled, " I want that wall opened. I don't care if you use axes, that wall has to be breached." She moved to a metal stairway that angled upward. "Where does this go to?" she asked, eyeing the hatch on the ceiling.

Jack followed Dasha's focus. "That's the access door to the roof. If there's a problem with any of the outside equipment that's how they get to it."

"Like what kind of equipment?"

"Vent motors, mostly."

Dasha turned around and sat down on the second step. "I'm not moving until there's a hole in that wall, and I get to see what's behind it."

Taking the suggestion as a command for action, Jack said, "I'll have a crew up here right away." He left and made his way toward the elevator.

Frank moved closer to Dasha. "I don't know if you saw it, but there's a red box near the elevator with a firehose and ax behind a glass door."

Dasha perked up. "Who knows how long it will take for that crew to get here. Have at it."

Frank returned, shouldering the ax like a woodsman intent on clearing a stand of trees. He went directly to the wall and gave it a few test hits with his fist to check its hollowness. He appeared to mentally mark the spot, then he followed through with a powerful stroke. The ax blade dug deep into the Sheetrock. He pulled back and took another stroke. Again the drywall yielded, and the crack widened.

Dasha got up from her roost and moved closer.

Blow after blow produced a deluge of facer and backer paper that clung to broken pieces of gypsum. With each stroke, clusters of pink insulation followed the tumbling fragments that grew larger at his feet. When spots of light began to show through the other side, Frank gave the wall a stout wallop. A backdraft of air, mixed with a shower of debris, surrounded him. "There's definitely something on the other side," he said, waving away the dust with his free hand.

The sound of the elevator door opening caused Dasha to redirect her attention.

The security guard, Jack, and an apparent maintenance worker, who was pushing a tool cart, their jaws agape, approached Dasha. "Well," the man in the coveralls began, "it looks like you made my job easier."

"That's rather risky," Jack said, pointing to the hole in the wall. "You could have run into some power lines."

131

"I guess we're lucky," Dasha snapped. She reached into her purse and pulled out her credentials and flashed them at Jack. "From now on this is a Central Consortium operation." She looked at the man holding onto the handcart. "I don't think we'll need your services, after all."

The workman, appearing bewildered, lingered awhile before he unhurriedly turning away and started for the elevator.

Dasha directed her attention back to Jack. "Beginning now, I want a guard stationed here until further notice. And no one, including the guard, is to go through that." She pointed at the opening. "Do you understand?"

Jack gave her a cold, distant nod. "Yes, Ms. Kozar."

Dasha turned back toward Frank, who'd just finished removing the last of the uneven pieces of plasterboard that extended beyond the metal studs. Although tight, the slit was sufficient to slip through

Meeting her impatient gaze, Frank made a hand gesture toward the opening. He said snidely, "After you, Ms. Kozar."

She shot him a look of disapproval and squeezed through the gap.

CHAPTER 45

Marcie eagerly returned to the couch. "I'm drained," she said with a grimace while massaging her abdomen.

Joe, standing nearby, saw that she was still in pain. "Want another ice pack?" he asked.

"No matter. I think I just need a little rest for now."

"Wouldn't the bed be more comfortable?"

"This is fine. You take the bedroom. I'm guessing you're as tired as I am."

"Before I turn in, I'll get something to cover you up." Joe located a throw in the linen closet, then caringly draped it over Marcie.

Marcie asked, "What good is this stuff without a way to connect them to a communications network?"

Joe softly kissed her forehead. She countered with a smile.

"Once everything is hooked up, I'll use the microwave transmitter from my old place to hotlink a pirated bandwidth allocation that I have been using for several years. I'm not really a hotlink hog, so my usage has remained low to avoid detection."

He could see Marcie's attention slowly fade away as she closed her eyes.

Joe considered her comment and looked around his safe house, troubled by the vast variety of equipment that needed to be hooked up. Although much of the infrastructure was in place, Joe calculated that his plan lacked one key element—that being time. He would need at least a couple of days but was unsure if even that was enough.

He began to shed his pilfered uniform and make his way toward the bedroom. Tomorrow was a new day, and his mind needed a break.

***

"Is that eggs and bacon I smell?" Marcie asked as she rose from the couch.

"I didn't think you wanted scotch for breakfast, so I slipped out for some provisions," Joe said while keeping a watchful eye on the stove. "Coffee is brewing if you're interested."

"Coffee and Molson, my two favorite drinks, but not together. I need to freshen up a bit first."

Joe gave a quick wave. "You know where the bathroom is. Breakfast will be ready in a few minutes, so you better hurry if you want to eat while it's hot."

When Marcie returned, Joe was already seated at the table. Marcie's breakfast, with swirls of steaming vapors, sat waiting for her. Joe said, "I guessed you would be eager to eat, so I didn't think you'd take too long in getting ready."

Marcie surveyed her plate. "That's a pretty substantial portion."

"I know, but let's face it, we haven't been eating well lately. Eat up."

Between bites, Joe studied Marcie. "When I told Dasha Kozar that you'd be going on a vacation for a few weeks with pay, that's before you clobbered that guard."

"You know, we didn't have much choice."

"No, don't get me wrong. You were right to have knocked him out, but I think the game has changed—not only the players."

"What do you mean?" Marcie asked between bites.

"I mean, we will be hunted and liquidated."

Marcie's fork paused in midair. "Oh, I never—"

"Yeah, I know, it's unsettling. But we're not alone. The consequence of their actions, just like ours, is capital punishment. The way the law is written, stealing from the Can-America Union is treason. They are operating outside of the law, and they will use any means available to get rid of us. By killing us will eliminate the potential for being caught. Right now there's no middle ground—it's either them or us."

Marcie continued to eat but at a slower pace. "What's your plan? I assume you have one?"

Joe motioned toward the array of equipment strewn about the living room. "I do. Today we connect this stuff. After that, we may have only one, or at best, two days to download the evidence against them. The problem will be in spreading the news of the crime. Keep in mind, they control the media. Nothing is published without their permission."

"That's a pretty sweet deal," said Marcie.

"Yeah ... something I haven't been able to work out yet." Joe eyed Marcie's nearly empty cup. "More coffee?"

She held it up toward him. "Please. And speaking about coffee, how did you manage to buy this food without leaving an E-pay trail?"

Joe filled Marcie's cup. "I have a fake E-account. The money is there, but the real holder of the account doesn't exist."

Marcie blew over the curl of steam from her cup. "What about CCTV cameras?"

"This is Old Town. The wiring feeds are outdated. Some work, while others have been purposely sabotaged by the residents living here. From the anti-government coalition, I have been notified of places to stay away from."

"A thought just occurred to me," Marcie said, her eyes wide with enthusiasm.

"What's that?"

"Once you find out the truth about Kozar and her allies, why can't you start a rumor among your network? Wouldn't the allegation gain some traction and cause an investigation by the government?"

Joe shook his head. "Remember that Central Consortium controls the news. They would counter with propaganda of their own and nullify the claim. Whatever we do has to be documented and released at once."

"No matter. I just thought—"

"No, that's okay. I know we'll eventually come up with an idea, but let's get going to put this equipment to work first."

CHAPTER 46

The interior of Joe's abandoned lair was dimly lit, and the negligible glow from the mechanical room edged its way at Dasha's heels. She felt her way along the walls in search of a control switch. "Victoria! Turn on the lights," she called out. Nothing happened until she moved beyond a laser-controlled beam that triggered soft, diffused illumination giving the interior a pleasing ambiance.

Frank, still silhouetted in the doorway, blinked as the room filled with a synthetic radiance. "Wow, I'm impressed," he said, scanning the inside.

Dasha stared at him with an intimidating look. "Remember, he's the enemy, and we're not here to praise his creativity. I want you to start gathering anything that will help us locate this Gary, or whatever he calls himself, and his whore."

Frank, his face flush with emotion, turned away and proceeded to cull through all the remnants of a hurried retreat. He picked up a small, wastepaper container. Before using it as a repository for anything of interest, he inspected its contents. Finding nothing of forensic value, he hastily discarded the scraps onto the floor. He hunted without comment, preferring to ruminate on Dasha's newly acquired frosty attitude.

Dasha, too, for the most part, remained silent, seemingly focused on the task at hand. Page after page was inspected and thrown about like unwanted handbills. Soon the floor became littered with portions of disjointed files and broken hardware. The occasional groan of annoyance slipped from her mouth, followed by a gale of whirling papers. Dasha immersed herself in a frenzy of discovery. Then, as the eye of the storm brings a curious calm, so did her furor suddenly cease.

"Humm," she said.

Frank took note of the unexpected lull. Mindful of her recent change in temperament he guardedly asked, "Find something?"

"Maybe," Dasha said quietly.

Without an invitation, Frank put aside his basket and joined her. He looked over her shoulder. "What's that?"

"An E-statement for a Wrey Williams."

"Who's Wrey Williams?"

"That's a good question. Why would this receipt be here?"

"Could he be an accomplice?" Frank asked.

Dasha pensively shook her head. "Not likely. It's either here because it was stolen and used for nefarious reasons, or Wrey Williams and Gary are one and the same." She waved the sheet in the air. "If this is really a list of all his transactions, then we have found the beginnings of the breadcrumb trail that's going to ultimately land him and his girlfriend into a jail cell."

"Do you want me to continue looking for other clues?"

Dasha carefully folded the paper and placed it in her purse. "No, I think we may have found the Rosetta Stone to all his activities. We'll go back to Central Consortium and have a team of our own people come back here to sift through this stuff. In the meantime, you and I will trace these account numbers." She patted the side of her purse. "Once we find out where and what is being purchased, we'll get a clearer picture of his operational sphere. Then we close in."

"So, you've changed your mind? You said he's going to land up in jail."

Dasha brushed past Frank on her way out. Speaking evasively, she said, "I was talking metaphorically."

CHAPTER 47

Joe finished connecting the last feed into the wall socket. "I have to say you really surprised me."

"How's that?" Marcie asked.

"I guess it's the way you seemed to know your way around electronics."

"Surprised because I'm a woman or surprised that I am, or I guess you could say I *was* a cleaning crew supervisor?"

Joe let out a sigh. "No, neither. You're intelligent, and that intelligence was obviously underutilized. Why you weren't encouraged to seek a higher position is beyond my understanding."

"I consider myself a free spirit and do what I want. You must know that's not a very admired trait in *The Company*. And isn't that true in your case, too?"

"Yes, but I'm not in *The Company*."

Marcie smiled. "So, I guess we are indeed two of a kind—apparently on opposite sides."

"I don't think that's the case anymore."

"You're right. We've joined forces."

Joe approached Marcie and held her in his arms. He looked into her welcoming eyes. "I thought we already had this conversation shortly after we met. I mean the part that we were made for each other."

"We did. I just like to hear it again." She drew closer and kissed him.

Still in their embrace, Joe said, "And if we want to stay together, we need to get on with the job of exposing the corruption within Central Consortium's organization."

Marcie pulled back. "You're right. If it's okay with you, I'd like to continue my research on the Brahe Project."

"That's fine," Joe said. "I think if we worked together on the lottery business, we'd get in each other's way." As an afterthought, he paused and considered her question again. "What's so interesting about an astronomy study?"

"First, the fact that it's coded and delivered with the high priority batch sparked my curiosity. The other reason was the considerable amount of data and corresponding addendums proving the hypothesis."

Joe shook his head. "I may be dense, or wasn't paying attention in school, but you never said anything about a hypothesis. What hypothesis are you talking about?"

"Well, we were in a bit of a hurry, and I guess it slipped my mind. What I have been able to discern so far is that the Brahe Project, in essence, was launched to map the entire universe."

"Yeah, I remember you said that the universe is made up of mostly dark matter. So what does Tycho Brahe have to do with the Brahe Project?"

"Based on what I have been able to extrapolate from these notes, Brahe became the first person to complete a star catalog. I guess somebody thought it was a good idea to name their project after someone who set out to map the then known universe of the sixteenth century."

Joe shrugged. "Interesting, but I need to get going on my project to prove that money is being siphoned off the lottery."

"No matter," Marcie said. "I have plenty to do to keep me occupied."

CHAPTER 48

Frank, feeling indifferent, grabbed one of the reports and moved to the side to study it. "This utility statement isn't from the same address as the apartment building."

Dasha, her desk overflowing with reports, leaned back into her chair with an aura of triumph. "Of course, it isn't," she mocked. "If that place had an address, it wouldn't be a secret. Somehow that bastard was getting his electric and water free of charge. No, that address is in Old Town. And if I'm correct in my speculation, that's where our rogue is hiding out."

Frank yawned. "So, is that where we are going?"

Dasha sprang from her chair, clapped her hands together with one sound slap, and moved to the window. She appeared driven. "Not tonight. Tonight we celebrate. Tonight we let our hair down, so to speak, and do Old Town—Bah-joo included."

Frank studied her, forced a smile then gazed beyond the window. "I remember the last time I had too much Bah-joo."

"It wasn't all bad, now was it, Frank?"

He avoided eye contact. Silent, he felt he was being exploited. Her recent manic mood swings made him reconsider if he had trusted the wrong person. Frank looked at the utility sheet again, then went to placed it back on Dasha's desk.

Dasha turned toward him. "What's a matter, Frank? I hope you're not going into one of your snits?"

Her question bothered him. He felt trapped. Ever since he met Dasha, she had controlled him—he was entirely dependent on her. He felt the room closing in on him. Frank moved back to the window, next to Dasha. He cursed the window for blocking him from leaping, head first, to the ground below. "I'm lonely," Frank said lethargically.

Dasha immediately shot him a questioning look. "Lonely? How can you be lonely? You have me?"

Her question hung uncomfortably in the air before he turned toward her. "I feel isolated from my past. I feel abandoned. I have this sense that I have been deposited on an island without remembering the voyage."

"Frank, you're overthinking again." She turned back to her desk and grabbed her purse. "Come on, let's go to Old Town and shake off those blues."

They walked past the now-empty cubicle cells, where only hours before, men like drone bees, labored under the total domination of an autocratic Tsarina, Samantha Brighton. Frank felt empathy with them because he knew he was one with them.

***

At the moment, content in the heart of Mr. Lau's Bar, Frank leaned back after finishing the last bite of his Kung Pao chicken. "I think its probably better to have something in one's stomach before having Bah-joo," he said.

"I'm glad to see your disposition has improved," Dasha said.

Although he felt better having his hunger satisfied, his wariness remained.

The beaded curtain shimmered and fluttered as the server pushed his way into their booth. "You done?" he asked, without displaying a hint of affability.

Dasha silently answered with a wave. As the plates were noisily collected, she said, "Two Bah-joo, Black."

Without any response, the man left.

"Not much of a talker," Frank said, his eyes watching the curtain undulate in the man's wake.

"The employees here at Mr. Lau's tend to mind their own business. This is a perfect spot for those who require privacy," Dasha answered warmly.

"Now that you know where that guy is hiding out, what's your plan?" Frank asked.

"My plan? *Our plan* is to eliminate the problem."

Once more, the curtains fluttered as their waiter returned with two drinks. He placed them on the worn table and promptly left.

Dasha lifted her glass. "To tomorrow and victory."

Frank reached for his drink. Drawing the glass close to his lips, he said indifferently, "To tomorrow," and took a token sip while Dasha drained her Bah-joo.

"That's no way to celebrate," Dasha said mockingly. "Drink up, or you'll bring us bad luck."

Reluctantly he bent to her pressure and consumed the entire Bah-joo in one swig. His stomach throbbed, and warmth radiated throughout his body, pausing in his brain. "A bit much at one time," he said, his face glowing.

"Waiter!" Dasha called out. "Two more Bah-joo, Black."

Frank waved a refusing hand. "I don't know. Remember the not so pleasant aftereffects of the following day."

"One more, Frank, then we'll call it a night. After all, we do need our sleep." She gave him a flirtatious wink.

They finished their second drink at a measured pace, making Frank more unreceptive to Dasha's deceptive charms. "When we eliminate the problem," he began, mindful of the inference, "what do we do next?"

"We?" she asked coldly.

"Yeah, you and me, what about you and me?" Franks's tone became more of a demand than a query.

"I told you before, you go on being an editor at the Central Consortium, and I ... well, I go on to my next assignment."

Frank cleared his throat. "That's what you said before we became involved. I thought that had changed in light of ... "

Dasha remained silent and played with her now empty glass.

Frank's own insecurity growled inside him. He felt betrayed. He could see she was avoiding his gaze. "I think it's time to leave," he said with wounded prickliness.

"Sure, we'll go back to your place, and I'll give you a nice body massage. That should loosen you up."

"No," he said forcefully. "I'll take a U-cab back to my apartment."

Dasha's jaw dropped. "It's not safe to walk the streets of Old Town by yourself. You'll need my protection." She patted her purse.

"I don't need your gun to protect me. I'll take my chances. " Frank immediately rose and faced Dasha. "I'll see you tomorrow morning. And don't come to my apartment to bother me until then." He turned and forcefully pushed back the bead-trimmed curtain.

CHAPTER 49

Marcie rubbed her eyes with the heels of her palms and stroked back her hair away from her face. She turned toward Joe, who remained focused on his monitor. "I need a break," she said quietly.

Joe nodded. "How about a nice cold Molson?"

"You have a Molson, and you kept it a secret?" she bristled.

Joe's smile was more sheepish than teasing. "I was afraid we wouldn't get anything done. That's why I hid it at the back of the refrigerator."

"Did you ever think I might work harder if I knew you had some?"

He laughed. "You don't expect me to believe that, do you?"

She snickered. "Well … maybe I would have."

"Sure, if you say so. We can squeeze in a break. Why don't you relax on the couch? I'll fetch the beers."

Joe returned and handed Marcie one of the bottles then sat alongside her on the floor next to the couch. He leaned back against the front of the sofa while resting his right hand on the seat cushion, beside Marcie.

"Are you ever going to tell me about your brother?" Marcie asked.

Joe took a sip of his beer. After the second swallow, he cleared his throat. "Okay." He began unhurriedly. "He was more than a brother, he was my twin."

Marcie let out a conspicuous breathe. "Oh," she said softly.

"We were alike in many ways—looks, interests, and personalities. Some might say that's unusual, but I guess we were unusual. The only difference happened to be Jim's desire to work for the government. I chose to fight against it. Jim respected my decision, and it was never a bone of contention between us."

"Was he married?"

"No. Jim thought that the Can-American union's *female-first-forever* policy made it difficult for him to support a wife. He assumed that if he were to marry, his wife would be expected to work in a career other than being a housewife. The tax penalties would have been too high, and the social pressure awkward."

"I understand," Marcie said. "In my case, it certainly has been to my advantage, but there still is discrimination based on social standing. I'm surprised he didn't follow your example."

"He was too easy-going for him to buck the system. Anyway, that proved to be his own undoing."

"How's that?"

"He became a building inspector and a very conscientious one. Knowing of my disdain for the government, he helped me carve out that private world I had up until a few days ago. He simply looked the other way and allowed me to create my hideaway."

"If he was such a government man, why did he do that for you?"

"Blood is thicker than governmental regulations. Long story short—he was older than me by two minutes. That made him feel responsible for me after our parents died in *The Great Upheaval*."

Marcie looked at Joe with astonishment. She appeared on the verge of saying something.

Joe interrupted the unsaid thought. "Another story for another time."

Marcie lightly touched Joe's arm.

"My brother's deception regarding my construction of a hideaway was probably his only deceitfulness. His integrity was tested when a government project neared completion, and he was asked to do a final inspection. Normally, the inspector remains with one project until completion. What happened to the original inspector with that project is a mystery. My brother, Jim, was told to rubber-stamp his approval and be done with it. It went against his grain. He refused."

"You said your brother was killed by CAS agents. Why would they get involved in a building project?" Marcie asked.

"They don't. CAS agents were called to that building site to investigate the death of my brother. He was found at the bottom of the elevator shaft, presumably having fallen to his death. It was listed as an accident."

"So far, what you have told me sounds routine. Why did you say CAS agents killed him?"

Joe took a full gulp from his bottle of beer. "Because the CAS agents changed the time of their arrival to one hour *after* they actually arrived."

Marcie gave Joe a dazed look. "How do you know that?"

"I was suspicious since Jim confided in me about the pressure he was under to approve the final inspection report. I reasoned that since his integrity couldn't be compromised, pressure was exerted on him to change his mind."

"That still doesn't tell me how you knew the time."

"I did some digging around, along with my partner. We found that the actual time the CAS agents arrived was documented on the CCTV security cameras from across the street."

Marcie bolted upright. "Getting information from you is a tiring task. Now, give it to me straight. Who's your partner and what did you and your partner actually do, besides run afoul of the law?"

Joe felt guilty. "You're right. I've been living an isolated life so long that it's difficult to be more open. Remember, our network is loosely connected to avoid major security breaches. At one time, I only had one partner. He was—"

"I remember now," Marcie interrupted. "and that—"

The motion alarm signaled an intruder. Joe sprang from his seated position on the floor and hurried to check the security camera. Seeing who it was, he grabbed his revolver and sprinted toward the entryway.

Marcie jumped off the couch and stood frozen, fixing her gaze on Joe.

Standing in wait, within the shadow of the hallway, Joe leveled his gun at the door.

CHAPTER 50

There was a hesitant knock on the door.

Joe held his position. He recognized his interloper, yet called out, "Who's there?"

The visitor did not counter with a reply.

Joe glanced back at the monitor and saw his caller standing in check, with hands reaching deep into his trenchcoat. The man looked drowsily in the direction of the security camera, his face furrowed with unease. Then, as if by an unspoken order, both hands sought freedom. With open palms, he faced them toward the door. He reached out and knocked again, then resumed a pose of surrender.

Keeping a firm grip on the revolver, Joe cautiously turned the double sets of deadbolts, then slowly opened the door. The light from the interior fell on Frank Fitzsimons, a.k.a. Rodney Bells. His hands remained open.

Joe shot a quick look beyond the evening caller, probing the gloom of the night, that may have concealed a confederate. Joe brandished his pistol and coaxed the man to enter. "Have a seat over there," Joe ordered, motioning toward a kitchen chair.

He complied and sat, his arms still raised in submission.

"Put 'em down," Joe ordered.

Slowly he obeyed and rested his hands on his lap.

Marcie moved toward the kitchen and leaned her back, with arms crossed over her chest, against the sink.

Joe tested the intruder. "What's your name?"

"Frank Fitzsimons, but I'm not certain it's really my name."

"Do you know me, Frank?" Joe quizzed again.

"If I do, I don't recall."

"Why are you here, and how did you find me?"

Frank looked apprehensively at Marcie then locked eyes with Joe. "I'm here to warn you that my ... my partner knows where you are. She got your address from an E-check statement."

Joe shot a quick look at Marcie. Looking at Frank again, he said, "I don't understand. Why are you here?"

"You know me, don't you? You called me Rodney at the overlook spot."

"I did," Joe said.

"I'm here because I want to know the truth about myself. Who am I?"

Joe slowly lowered his weapon and sat down on a nearby chair. An overwhelming feeling of compassion swept over him. He looked at Rodney not as an adversary, but as a damaged individual, broken by the state for the sole purpose of exploitation. "I'll tell you, but I'm not sure you'll remember."

"I need to know."

***

Rodney Bells buckled under the weight of Joe's account. Hunching over, he pondered the floor. No longer Frank Fitzsimons, he asked, "Did I have a wife or girlfriend?"

"No," Joe replied softly.

Rodney examined Joe, hoping to see a thread of recognition in his face that would help mend his fractured life. He only saw pity. Turning away, Rodney cupped his chin in his hands. "What do I do now?" he asked, deep inside wishing for a painless answer.

"Rod," Joe began, "that's what I used to call you. I think the simple solution would be for you to go back to your apartment. Dasha will most certainly pick you up tomorrow, and I would guess come here."

He shrugged. "Then what?"

"Honestly, I don't know. So only you, Dasha and Samantha Brighton know about me?"

Rodney nodded. "Yeah, for some reason they did not want CAS agents involved."

"I can now tell you why," Joe said and grabbed a folder off the side table. He opened it and pulled out a sheet of paper. Waving it toward Rodney, he said, "I just finished confirming my suspicions. This report proves that Dasha Kozar, a.k.a., Charlotte Piper and Samantha Brighton, a.k.a., Amelia Clark are partners in defrauding the lottery of millions of Crypto credits."

Rodney shook his head in disbelief. "So, Dasha and Samantha are—"

"Yeah ... lovers," Joe said matter-of-factly. "And not only are they involved romantically, but their control over the media also makes them extremely powerful."

"That explains why they're so intent on silencing you."

"Yeah, and now that I know, I'll be ready."

Rodney's mind raced with visions of a bloody confrontation, with no clear winner. "You'll be a sitting duck—your hideout, nothing more than a trap of your own making."

Joe rose from his chair and motioned toward the exit. "You're free to go, Rod."

"How do you know that I won't say something to Dasha?"

"I just know," Joe said, and coaxed Marcie to his side. "The very act of you coming here to warn us is proof enough. I don't understand what the government did to your brain, but I believe the goodness is still there." Joe put his arm around Marcie. "Just go back to your place and let us handle the rest."

Rodney Bells felt relieved. Mentally shedding the identity of Frank Fitzsimons, he opened the door and walked into the beginning of his new life.

CHAPTER 51

"Where did you go last night?" Dasha asked Frank as they drove to the Central Consortium's headquarters.

"Nowhere," Frank replied bluntly. He found it difficult to hide his emotional state considering his liberation and newly discovered identity.

"Nowhere? You weren't with me, so you had to have gone somewhere."

The physical Frank was there, but Rodney Bells unintentionally studied the blurred landscape as they raced along with the morning traffic. Without turning his head toward Dasha, he said softly, "I needed to clear my head. I just walked and walked."

"Hum," Dasha responded with a hint of unmistakable suspicion in her tone.

Frank, not wanting to continue with her train of questioning, asked, "If you know where this guy is hiding out, why are we going to headquarters?"

"I want to run everything through Ms. Brighton first. Besides, she doesn't want phone communications … everything has to be face-to-face."

Frank said, "Anything new from the apartment hideout?"

"I'll find out more when I talk with her."

"Don't you mean *we*?"

His question hung uncomfortably without a rejoinder.

"Dasha?"

She cleared her throat. "Brighton wants me to speak with her alone."

Frank wanted to explode with accusations and divulge what he knew. Instead, he let her remark go unchallenged and resumed his indifferent review of traffic.

***

Brighton closed her polarizing drapes when Dasha entered her office, She moved eagerly toward Dasha, embraced her, and gave her a passionate kiss. "Have a seat and tell me what you've learned so far," Brighton said, then promptly returned to her desk and took a seat. She appeared rejuvenated.

"They think they're so smart, but we located them in Old Town."

Sitting comfortably in her throne of power, Brighton said, "I knew something was up when I received word that you wanted our investigative team to check out his hideaway." She shook her head. "And of all places … right inside my apartment building."

"Have you heard anything from them?" asked Dasha.

"Yes. Although the computers were removed, there's a paper trail of this Gary Duprey's treacherous deeds. I'm sure you'll agree, any attempt to involve CAS will undoubtedly prove an embarrassment to us."

"I figured as much. I don't think we can wait too long before we act."

"What are you suggesting?" asked Brighton.

"I'm going to take care of the problem by the end of the day."

Brighton's eyes narrowed. "What about Frank? Is he okay with the plan?"

"I think he's getting a little squeamish. I'm not certain that procedure isn't without complications."

"What do you mean?" Brighton asked.

"Suffice it to say, residual memory may hamper complete submission. I'm not a doctor, but I don't think it's foolproof."

"What about after the assignment?"

Dasha rested her elbows on her chair's armrest, folded her hands like in prayer, and placed her chin on her thumbs. She spoke into the hollow of her palms. "He's too much of a liability." She dropped back into the chair while lowering her arms. "I'm sure you'll agree on what we need to do?"

Brighton did a slow, pensive nod. "I agree."

CHAPTER 52

"It's getting late," Frank said. "Maybe they have stocked their place with food and won't come out for several days. We can't stay here forever."

"I've tracked their purchases under the assumed E-account. They didn't buy that much. Just like rats, they'll be coming out of their hole tonight. You can count on it."

Frank pointed toward Dasha's purse that rested on the car's dash. "If you plan on using that, there will be noise, and the local cops will swarm over this area. I don't care how powerful you are, using a gun in any crime will result in a trip to Toronto, and you know what will happen. Just being with you makes me an accomplice."

Dasha, stony-faced, stared at Frank with contempt. "Listen, I have a noise suppressor for it, and the gun's unregistered. If we have to use it, we're both wearing gloves so our fingerprints won't be on it. Also, so far as doing a hit … this is Old Town."

Frank sat uneasily in his seat, uncertain of Dasha's strategy. As time dragged on, his concerns lessened that there would be a confrontation this night. The prolonged inaction lulled him into sleepiness. On the verge of nodding off, Frank sensed Dasha stiffen to readiness.

"Frank, look," she whispered. Across the narrow alleyway,and a block away, a sliver of light escaped from the unlocked door, backlighting the couple for only a few seconds. When they finally moved into the street, they became partially bathed in the yellowish glow from a nearby streetlamp. Their subdued outlines moved unhurriedly onto the roadway.

Dasha engaged the car. With her headlights turned off, she floored the accelerator. Despite being blended within the shadows, Frank could see Joe and Marcie freeze. Joe appeared surprised. Coming out of his momentary paralysis, Frank observed Joe attempting to push Marcie clear.

Frank, stunned by Dasha's coldness, instinctively, grasped the steering wheel and yanked it from her grip. She stared at him with hard eyes and tried to regain control. "What the hell's wrong with you?" she shouted.

Before Frank could respond, he felt the impact. The car came to a screeching halt before hitting the building behind Marcie. Frank's seatbelt strained under the sudden stop. The strap tightened and jerked him back into his seat.

"You bastard!" Dasha yelled, and her eyes pierced him with contempt. She fumbled for her purse, reached in, and pulled out her M-17. Coiling her gloved hands around the lower receiver, she began to train the gun on Frank.

Frank grabbed Dasha's wrists, and pushed back. Three muffled shots went wild and pierced the roof of the car. While keeping her in check with one hand, he used his other to punch the side of her head. She looked dazed and disorientated. Her grip loosened on the pistol. Frank attempted to pull the weapon from her. Two more shots were fired, shattering the rear window. In a wild frenzy, he hit her again and again. Grabbing the pistol's grip, he wrenched the gun from her hands. His finger became locked inside the handgun's trigger guard. Dasha forcibly pulled on the firearm's upper receiver. Her face exploded.

The acrid smell of expended gunpowder filled the car's tight compartment. Pumped with adrenaline, Frank's hands shook, and his ears felt as if they would explode. He stopped and pondered the gruesome aftermath and Dasha's lifeless body. Breathing deeply and in shock, he turned away from the blood-spattered interior. He observed someone approach and cried out, "Joe?"

Uncertain he was heard, Frank cracked open the car's door. He called out again, "Joe?" He stumbled free of the carnage. His unsteady legs barely held him erect as he stepped onto the road.

Joe grabbed the top of the car door and helped Frank to his feet. "You okay, Rod?"

Bewildered, Frank gradually came to his senses and acknowledged his new moniker. Frank, a.k.a. Rodney Bells slowly nodded.

"Good," Joe said and assisted the resurrected Rodney Bells from the automobile. "Marcie's been badly hurt. We have to get her back into my apartment."

"Won't the police know where you are?"

Joe led Rodney away from the car. "Not if we get going before anyone comes onto the scene. This area is mostly businesses and warehouses. Not much traffic this time of the night, but we have to move *now*."

Rodney saw Marcie sprawled onto the roadway. Writhing in pain, her groans suggested her injury was life-threatening, yet, besides the scuff mark on the side of her head, she was not bleeding.

"Rod, give me a hand and let's get her inside."

"Joe, it may not be safe to move her if she's got a spinal injury."

Rodney could see Joe was near tears.

"I know, I know, but I can't leave her. Help me. We have to take a chance."

Rodney removed his bloodstained gloves and shoved them into his jacket pocket. Joe and Rodney squatted down, joined their hands under Marcie, forming a human chair, and then lifted her. Marcie, still conscious, moaned in agony as they spirited her away.

Getting as far as the front door, Joe grew unnerved.

"Don't worry, I have her," Rodney shouted. "Hurry, get the door."

Unlocking the door, Joe guided Rodney, who strained under the weight of Marcie, into the bedroom. Joe then helped ease her onto the bed. Every movement, no matter how slight, produced an anguished outburst from Marcie's lips.

"You take care of Marcie," Rodney said. "I'll go and make sure we didn't leave a trail back to this place."

***

Joe felt Marcie's weak pulse. Touching her arm he noted that her skin was cold and clammy. He gathered the blankets from the foot of the bed and covered her. He then took the two pillows that were at the head of the bed and positioned them under Marcie's legs. He ran into the other room.

As Joe rummaged through the linen closet, the outside door opened. Rodney arrived holding the M-17. He closed the entrance to the approaching sound of a siren. "I don't believe anything will lead the police here," Rod said nervously. He waved the gun in the air. "I didn't think it was a good idea to leave this behind. How's Marcie doing?"

"She's in shock." With hands full of blankets, Joe rushed back into the bedroom.

Rodney followed and saw that Marcie was having difficulty breathing. Her deathly pallor told him that it was serious. A trickle of blood dripped from the corner of Marcie's mouth.

After spreading the covers over Marcie, Joe knelt along the side of the bed and stroked her matted hair. He started to cry.

Marcie's eyes flickered as she turned toward Joe. "The Brahe Project ... Joe, you must publish the Brahe Project."

Publish? He thought she was delirious. "Don't worry about that, now. You'll be all right. Just rest." Within his mind, he knew differently. He had trapped them both.

"Joe," she whispered, "I love you."

Through tears and intermittent sniffles, he said, "I love you, too. You'll be all right. You'll be all right."

"No matter," she said, then forced a weak smile and her eyes rolled back into an eternal stare. Her jaw relaxed as she breathed her last.

Joe buried his face into his hands and inconsolably wept.

Rodney reached over and closed Marcie's eyelids. He then placed a rolled towel under her slackened chin and left Joe to his grieving.

CHAPTER 53

As soon as Joe walked through the doorway of the bedroom, he felt drained. He looked not at Rodney, but at the pulsing light from the emergency vehicles that spilled out through the gaps in the shutters. He moved toward the kitchen counter and considered the M-17.

"What are you thinking? Rodney asked.

"I'm going to kill every one of those sons-of-bitches," he barked.

Rodney rose from his chair and met him face on. He stood between him and the gun. "You don't have enough bullets to do that. Besides, there are other ways to get back at them."

"Like what?"

There was pounding at the door. "Go, get in the bathroom," Joe ordered. He looked at the gun resting on the counter and hastily threw a towel over it.

More pounding at the door.

"Coming!" Joe yelled.

Once Rodney was out of sight, Joe opened the entrance door.

Two burly cops clad in body armor greeted Joe. "Hello, citizen," one of the men said. "There has been an accident a block away from your apartment."

"Oh?" Joe acted stunned.

"Did you see or hear anything unusual tonight?"

"I was on the couch, sleeping. Anything serious, officer?"

Ignoring the question, one of the officers looked closely at Joe. "Your eyes are swollen. Is there something wrong?"

"Allergies."

He appeared to consider Joe's explanation, then said, "Citizen, may we see your identification?"

While one of the men looked over Joe's false credentials, the other policeman produced an ultraviolet light-wand. "Citizen, show us your arms, palms up, please," he demanded.

Joe complied and extended them. The light turned his skin dull and patchy. The wand followed the contours of his arms.

"Now the other side, sir."

Again Joe obeyed.

"Citizen, please roll up your sleeves."

Now bare, once more his arms were scanned. Apparently satisfied with the results, they issued an apology and thanked Joe for his cooperation.

Joe waited until the police were gone before telling Rod the coast was clear. "They scanned me for blood residue. We're okay for now," he said lethargically. He went over to the couch to lay down and stared at the ceiling.

With a shaky voice, Rodney asked, "What about Marcie?"

Without making eye contact, Joe said, "I don't know." His eyes began to well up. "She deserves a proper funeral, yet I can't bring myself to part with her."

Rodney sighed. "I think I can help."

Still looking up at the ceiling, Joe asked, "How's that?"

"In the short period that I worked for Central Consortium, I made contacts with other agencies."

Joe shot him a sideways glance. "Like who?"

"The Bureau of Missing Persons."

"How are they going to help?"

Rod shifted in his chair. "They have refrigeration units that store unidentified bodies for a short period."

After a protracted silence, Joe asked, "How long?"

"Long enough for us to take down Samantha Brighton."

Joe studied the ceiling again. "I don't know. I can't think. If it weren't for me, Marcie would still be alive." He began to weep.

Rodney got up from his chair and went back into the bathroom. He removed his bloodstained jacket and shirt, then washed his face and hands. After drying himself, Rodney looked down and noticed his slacks were also stained. He returned to the living room and saw that Joe had regained some control over his grief. "Joe, do you have any extra clothes that would fit me?"

"Yeah, I think so, but they might be a little on the loose side. "Joe listlessly got up off the couch and went toward the bedroom.

"Hold on a second," Rod said. "Let me go in there first." When he did enter, he took one of the bedsheets and draped it over Marcie's body. He called back to Joe. "You can come in now."

Joe gave the shrouded body a quick look and hurried toward the closet. He flung open the door. "Help yourself," he said somberly and immediately left the room, this time avoiding even a stolen glance at the bed.

When Joe came back into the kitchen, he was wearing a black sweatshirt with jeans. He saw Joe standing near the countertop, studying the M-17, but without handling it.

"You're not ... " Rodney trailed off.

Joe shook his head. "I just don't know what to do. I've never loved anyone as much as I loved Marcie."

Rod moved toward Joe and put a consoling hand on him. "Let me handle everything. We're going to have to produce the evidence against Brighton. I think you should get all that stuff together while I take care of Marcie."

With hunched shoulders, Joe moved toward the computers. "Yeah, you're right. I need to focus."

"I'm curious," Rodney began, "what's so special about the Brahe Project?"

"I don't know. Marcie took it upon herself to get involved with it. It's something about astronomy. It was sort of a hobby of hers."

"She seemed pretty insistent," Rodney said.

"I think Marcie became delirious at the end. I have all my proof I need to expose Samantha Brighton and Dasha Kozar's corruption. I'll take a peek at her notes later."

"I have an idea that we'll only have one shot at this," Rodney said. "And tomorrow morning may be our only chance for success."

CHAPTER 54

"Are you ready?" Rodney Bells, a.k.a. Frank Fitzsimons asked as he straightened his tie.

"As ready as I'll ever be, even though I hardly slept a wink last night," Joe said sluggishly.

"Marcie?" Rodney asked softly.

"Yeah, I can't concentrate. It's hard stuffing my grief, but the Brahe Project ... "

Rodney looked at Joe with interest. "I thought it was just some hobby stuff. What's so special about it now?"

"I'm troubled by what she found."

"You're not going to tell me it's more important than pilfering from the lottery, are you?"

"I think so," Joe said uneasily.

"Well, are you going to tell me?"

Joe grabbed the M-17 off the counter. He put it in his briefcase, positioned the load under his arm, and walked to the full-length mirror. Checking himself, he asked, "I'm a bit nervous. How do I look?"

"Like a normal businessman," Rodney said with a tone of annoyance. "Now, are you going to tell me what the Brahe Project is all about?"

"Yeah, in the car on the way to Central Consortium's headquarters."

***

"So, what do you think?" Joe asked as he guided the car through the morning traffic.

Rodney stared blankly ahead. "You're right. It's hard to grasp. I'm not an astronomer or even a scientist, so it's hard for me to comprehend. Given a chance, how are you going to use that information?"

"Rod, today is the day we both make history. We have two stories to break—one to bring down Brighton and the other to bring down Can-America."

"Are you certain your plan will work?"

"We'll have the element of surprise. That's why we have to get there before Samantha Brighton."

Their car began to follow the string of other vehicles that turned into the Central Consortium's underground parking facility.

As they got out of the car, both men straightened their suits. After adjusting his own ID, Rodney Bells, now back as Frank Fitzsimons, inspected Joe. "Here," he said, grabbing the encapsulated employee badge that was tethered around Joe's neck, "let me fix that. You want everyone to think you belong here. And another thing, I know it's been tough on you, but you have to get rid of that frown. Once we're done, you can call them all assholes."

Joe forced a smile.

"Yeah, that's better, now let's give 'em hell."

Frank Fitzsimons and his partner, Roger Willcox, a.k.a. Joe Quin walked hurriedly among the stream of other employees. A few of the personnel gave them a passing glance. *Maybe our vindictiveness is showing,* Frank thought.

Because of the security coding on their badges, they were able to skip the complete body scan and proceed, unchallenged, through the checkpoint. When they got to the twentieth floor, even the receptionist was absent from his post.

Both men looked up at the bronzed crest over the entrance that bore the axiom, "Science is Truth, and only through DNA do we exist."

Joe Quin gave Frank a wry smile.

"Follow me," Frank said as he began to lead Joe through the labyrinth of workspaces and to his office. When they arrived, Frank anxiously checked the room, looking for any hint that his recent exploit compromised his standing with the agency. He turned on his computer and entered his passcode. It was accepted. He turned toward Joe. "Okay, this is it. Now we take on Brighton."

With quickened steps, they reached Samantha Brighton's office. Standing at her desk, she was sorting some correspondence when Frank and Joe burst into her room.

Brighton looked up in alarm, dividing her attention between the intruders. "What's this all about? Where's Ms. Kozar?"

Joe reached into his briefcase, pulled out the M-17 with its noise suppressor attached, and aimed it at Brighton. He used his briefcase as a shield against unwelcomed notice by any other employees. "Darken your windows," he ordered.

Brighton reached under her desk for the control.

"You better not hit any alarm switch, because it will be the last sound you'll hear," Joe said.

"What do you want and where is Ms. Kozar?' she demanded contemptuously.

"She's dead," Frank said.

Brighton looked shocked. With trembling hands, she felt for her chair and collapsed onto it. With a quaking voice, she asked, "How?"

Frank moved closer and sat in a nearby chair. "She's dead, that's all you need to know. Never mind how it happened, your days of stealing are over," he said while sliding a sheet of paper toward her.

The phone on Brighton's desk lit up. She began to reach for it, but stopped and looked at Joe.

Joe's gun bobbed. "Answer it, but one wrong word and it'll be your last."

"Hello … Brighton here," she said with an unsteady voice.

There was a long pause.

"Yes. Yes."

Another pause

"When did it happen?"

Slowly Brighton's face contorted into grief.

"I understand. Call me if I can be of any assistance." She hung up and glared at Joe. "You bastard!" she shouted. "You killed her, you bastard!"

"Shut up!" Frank ordered. "Read this." He put his hand once more on the sheet of paper."

Keeping her eyes on Joe, she fumbled for the sheet. She looked at it with marginal curiosity, then refocused her attention back to it. She hurriedly looked it over. "I'm not going to sign this." She flipped the document away. It drifted onto the floor and out of her sight.

Frank got up, retrieved it, and banged it back on her desk. "We don't want you to sign it. That's the script that will be read during the evening news," he said mockingly.

"Never!" she screamed.

"Oh, you will, and here's the deal." Frank paused while he waited for Brighton to calm down. "I'm going to go into my office, and you're going to call me with today's release code."

"And if I refuse?"

"The story will be released to CAS."

Brighton forcibly exhaled. "What's the difference? Either way, I'm beaten."

Frank picked up the paper and placed it on his lap. "Here's the deal. You give me the code I need to <u>send</u> the release to the network, and you'll have until six to escape. It's early now, and the longer you wait, the less time you have to split."

Brighton pushed herself back into her chair and crossed her arms over her chest. She appeared to think over the offer. "Frank, I never liked you from the beginning. I told Dasha that she shouldn't trust you." She paused and glanced at her watch. "Okay, you win."

Frank sprung from his chair. "Give me five minutes to log onto the system, then call me and give me today's release code."

In Frank's absence, Joe sat in his chair, keeping a watchful eye on Brighton. He rested the M-17 on his lap and covered it with the briefcase. Not one word was exchanged between them.

When Frank returned, Joe got up and resumed his combative attitude.

"It's done," Frank said. "As promised, you're free to take off after we leave." He approached Brighton's desk and lifted her secure phone. Using a pair of wire snips, he cut her line. "I'm not taking any chances that you'll rescind the order. Get up," he demanded. "Turn around and put your hands behind your back."

"This wasn't part of the deal," Brighton bristled.

"It really is," Frank said. "We're no fools. We start walking out of this place, and you'll have security all over us. Now, put your hands behind your back."

She scowled at him. "You told me that I could escape before the evening news telecast."

"Don't worry. These handcuffs will be attached to a timed lock. They'll release in fifteen minutes. You'll have plenty of time to skip town. Now, let's get on with it."

He snapped the cuffs on Brighton's wrists, secured a cabled lock to them and attached it to a building stanchion. "When the timer releases you, you'll need this to unlock the cuffs." He placed the key on a cabinet far away from Brighton's reach.

"Don't think you're going to walk away from this," Brighton warned. "I don't know which one of you killed Dasha, but murder is a capital offense."

"Oh, yeah, thanks for reminding me." Joe ejected the clip on the M-17 and laid it on Brighton's desk. He removed a cloth from his pocket and thoroughly wiped the magazine and then the gun. Joe grabbed the weapon, leaving the safety on, and made Brighton touch it along with the clip. He reassembled it and shoved it into one of the desk's drawers. He gave her a killing glare. "Frank told me it was your gun in the first place, so I suspect your fingerprints are all over those bullets."

Brighton's eyes stabbed back at him.

"One more thing," Joe said. He went behind Brighton and muzzled her mouth with a neckerchief. He yanked the ends tightly before tying the knot. "Just in case you should get the idea of yelling for help." He let out a derisive laugh.

Leaving her office, Frank pushed in the locking mechanism on the door before closing it.

Once on the ground floor, Frank and Joe made their way through the arched portico and toward the fountain of the nine Muses. They caught sight of a flood of CAS agents streaming in from the parking structure.

Joe hesitated.

Frank kept his pace. He called back to Joe. "Come on. They're not coming for us."

Several CAS agents rushed past, never taking the slightest interest in them.

"What's that all about?" Joe asked.

"That's your revenge for Marcie," Frank said. "If I didn't give Brighton some hope that she could escape the punishment, we wouldn't have been able to pull this off."

"How did you notify them?"

"When I sent the script to the network, I made a call to CAS headquarters."

Hurrying along the path to the garage, Joe asked, "And the Brahe Project? Marcie wanted that published."

"We'll catch it on the evening news," Frank said with a smile.

CHAPTER 55

No longer assuming the identity of Frank Fitzsimons, Rodney Bells and his old partner Joe Quin sat in Joe's new safe house apartment. Spartan by Joe's previous standards, it provided them with a new base of operation. Both men were resting on matching comfortable chairs, casually sipping on bottles of Molson beer.

Not looking directly at Rodney, but trained on the wallscreen television, Joe asked, "So, what are your plans?"

Rodney shrugged. "I haven't the slightest idea. I was kind of expecting you would help me with that. I think we should resume our partnership."

They traded glances.

"I was hoping you would say that. I'm still coping with the loss of Marcie," Joe said. "I want to give her a proper burial."

"Don't worry, I'll help you with that," Rodney said consolingly. "I assume you're going to fill me in on my past life?"

"We have a lot to talk about." Joe raised his bottle in a toast.

Rodney countered with a wave of his bottle.

They turned their attention back to the television.

Perera and her co-host, Zoe, dressed in matching red body-hugging costumes, emphasizing their perfect shapes, sauntered onto the center of their newsroom set.

"Well, we have some shocking news to announce," Zoe began.

"Yes," Perera agreed. "We have received confirmation that Samantha Brighton, the Central Consortium's head of telecommunications, has committed suicide."

Joe and Rodney froze, then glanced at each other in disbelief. They both moved to the edge of their seats.

"Sources within the agency said she's presumed guilty in a scheme to defraud the Can-American government. Government officials did not disclose the exact nature of the offense. Her accomplice, Dasha Kozar, also a high-ranking government official, was found murdered. Preliminary findings indicate that Samantha Brighton is the killer."

"Suicide?" Rodney asked aloud.

Joe slowly shook his head. "Maybe, but I doubt it. If she were allowed to tell her whole story, it would have undermined the confidence in the government. She would become toxic."

"So, you think …?

Joe nodded. "I'm pretty sure they made it look that way."

The camera focused on Zoe, who appeared distressed. "In other news, we have received a report from the scientific community that will no doubt have far-reaching consequences."

"This is it," Rodney said with pleasure. "I got it past the censors."

Zoe continued. "Known as the Brahe Project, it was initiated nearly a century ago—its purpose to map the universe. Using the spectra of light from distant galaxies, radio wave transmissions, and the effect of dark energy, it was discovered that the source of the universe isn't from the center because the universe has no center."

The view switched to Perera. "No center?" she asked in surprise. "Everything has a center."

The camera went back to Zoe. The expression on her face telling. "I don't understand it myself, Perera." There was tension in her voice. "But the source of the universe is … on the outside. The report goes on to say that it's like someone pulling in all directions on a huge bubble that has a myriad of interconnected clusters."

"Someone?" Perera asked off-camera.

The intricacy of the script appeared to be too much of a challenge for Zoe to continue. Apparently, in frustration, she blurted, "Like God."

The broadcast, abruptly terminated, faded to black.

ABOUT THE AUTHOR

Christopher Malinger lives with his wife Eileen, in Central Florida. His works include, *The Object of Desire*, which appeared in *Journeys VII*; an Anthology of Award-Winning Short Stories, published in 2014. Also, he was a winner in the Florida Writers Association's Adult Collection, Volume 7, *The Sweet Scent of Spring; published in 2015*. And again in 2017, his short story, *Iggy,* was included in the 2017 Florida Writers Association's Adult Collection. In 2018 he was voted one of the top ten writers in the Florida Writers Association's Adult Collection, Volume 10, for his short story, *A Story Teller's Tale.*

Other works include *Cat's Paw,* a fictional account of the bombing of British European Airline's Flight 284, published in 2016. A collection of short stories, *Tales to Keep You Awake, The Back Roads of Terror,* and his novella, *The Wabele,* which won second place for general fiction in the 2017 annual Florida Writers Association Royal Palm Literary award's contest.
In 2019, *Scrubbed* received the Silver Award (at the time) for the unpublished novella category.

He is a member of the Florida Writers Association.

www.ingramcontent.com/pod-product-compliance
Lightning Source LLC
Chambersburg PA
CBHW060418260626
47161CB00005B/1681